HELL'S KITCHEN

(From where everyone is served)

By:
David J. Miller

Bookman LLC
Publishing & Marketing

Providing Quality, Professional Author Services

www.BookmanMarketing.com

ISBN: 1-59453-265-6

Disclaimer

This novel is a work of fiction. The persons, secular-clergy-medical, and otherwise, and their professional positions, as well as the events portrayed, are products only of the author's imagination. Also corporations, businesses, medical diagnosis, and anatomical concepts are entirely fictional and are products of the author's imagination. Certain locations mentioned in this novel actually exist, but the events portrayed as occurring at those places are fictional. Any resemblance to actual persons (living or dead) events, locales, corporation or businesses is entirely coincidental.

Chapter One

It's nine o'clock in the morning as Father David Sheridan files through the cafeteria at St. Jonathan's hospital. With three others in line it'll only be a few minutes before he's able to settle down to a meager breakfast of oatmeal and black coffee. As the good Father makes his way through the dining room he notices an empty table adjacent to an open window, and thinks the crisp spring air will go well with the meal. It's been a busy night and an early morning, two last rites and a crisis on labor and delivery, all of which has worn this man out. Twenty-four hours without sleep will have an effect on anyone, and the hospital food he's about to eat will surely establish the predictability of his day. As some people dream of far off vacations Sheri is compensated by cataloged memories of former culinary

1

delights, always giving him hope for another, and may explain the thirty pounds he's lost. Then as he finishes his coffee the intercom announces. "Father David Sheridan, please pick up the red courtesy phone." From where he's sitting, the telephone looks as if it were two hundred yards away, distance is one thing, his energy level was another. Sheri now repositions the chair he was sitting in to match the table then begins walking in the direction of the house telephones all the while saying to himself, "Please give me a break there's nothing left." As duty demands Sheri retrieves the handset, saying, "Hello, Father Sheridan speaking."

"Sheri, Brian Farmsworth."

Brian's voice delivers a blow to the padre's second wind, not to mention his ego, leaving him speechless. The only thing going through Sheri's mind is how Farmsworth would go out of his way to make him feel uncomfortable at every opportunity, especially after returning to the seminary from their summer vacations. Brian would then proudly display his seasoned tan, usually acquired on the deck of a boat or on the tennis court, then inquire as to Sheri's vacation at the freight terminal, always with shallow overtones. Even to this day Sheri has a difficult time dealing with Farmsworth, because both men are aware they're at the opposite ends of the social ladder, with Brian retaining a certain privileged mentality which allows him to put his eight hours in, after which he's on his own. Sheri on the other hand had been accustomed to overtime, and to him it really didn't matter. He would stay behind to finish a project, because he knew everything in life was important, and if something had to be done he was certain there was a reasonable explanation that didn't need his prior approval.

"Yes Brian, how can I be of help to you or Bishop O'Daly?"

Farmsworth being the Bishop's assistant is quick and to the point. "John has asked that I arrange a meeting for this afternoon and wants you in attendance. Can you make it here by three o'clock?"

Sheri responds in an obedient fashion, saying, "I'll be there."

With the conversation having ended Sheri walks to his living quarters behind the chapel and begins to wonder what O'Daly's intentions are, or better yet what was Farmsworth up to. With his judgement now clouded with negativity he opts for a hot shower and a few hours sleep thinking he'd be clean and clear headed when he meets with O'Daly.

It's ten o'clock before Sheri is able to crawl between the covers, and as luck would have it there seems to be only a few

3

minutes in passing before the telephone rings. As he looks over at the clock Sheri realizes it's nearly three o'clock in the afternoon, and he hadn't moved a muscle in five hours, and wonders if this is an inquiry as to his whereabouts. Sheri now realizes those concerns will be addressed as he hears Farmsworth voice breaking the silence.

"Sheri what in the world is going on? You're supposed to be here in Albany by now. Listen, we're running late ourselves, I'll have to arrange a dinner meeting here at the office, that way you and the Bishop can discuss matters. I have to hurry now, don't let me down, and remember be here at the office by six o'clock."

With the conversation ending so abruptly Sheri's left holding the telephone receiver with no one on the other end of the line, leaving him feeling frustrated, and bewildered. In all the years he's known Farmsworth this is the first time Brian has gone out of his way to help Sheri. There's something going on where he's needed Sheri thinks, otherwise they would had used this delay against him. With this new insight Sheri begins to relax, using the hour and half before he's to leave to review his manuscript that's hidden under yesterday's newspaper. With the bound volume in hand Sheri reclines in his leather mission chair to tackle the task at hand, comfortably in place the title now blazes across the front page. The Forensic Study of Exorcisms, it's been two and a half years arriving to where it is now, and as anyone will tell you the chore begins with the turning of the first page, and ending with the last, with everything in between open to constructive criticism.

Sheri breaks his concentration long enough to look at the clock sitting next to his bed and realizes it's nearly four thirty, he'll have to put this aside. There's no time to spare, he needs to secure the chapel and make the trek outside of the building where a reserved parking spot protects his 1964 Chevy Camero. Yes, after thirty years he and the car are still together, and with arrangements being made every winter to store his prize away from the salt, and road hazards he's reasonably sure they'll be together for sometime to come.

With the turn of the key and the thrill of the drive calling out Sheri is finally able to experience the freedom of the road. With the sun to his back he now has an Easterly heading, it'll be just a few more miles before he reaches the New York Interstate where they'll be nothing between him and the meeting except time and space. As the miles pass tranquillity assumes its position as Sheri's companion, freeing him from the anxiety of the trip. While adjusting to this sensation his attention is drawn to the dashboard where the clock is now registering five-thirty. There's only enough time to drive the remaining twenty miles he thinks, and then another ten minutes to O'Daly's office. With

Farmsworth's warning now becoming an irritation the next twenty minutes pass with an unspoken urgency leaving Sheri wondering what he's to expect. Although yesterday was hectic, things had been somewhat predictable, however this evening is another matter, it'll be Church politics and that'll be a toss of the coin.

As Sheri makes a right turn onto the off ramp the pager attached to his belt is activated by an incoming call. He looks down and notices the time as being five-fifty five and the number as that registered to the diocesan office. While driving into the parking lot he senses that Brian is beginning to panic. Scanning the second floor he sees Farmsworth standing on the balcony in somewhat of an anxious state, and looking tense enough to launch into space. Sheri begins to laugh, then blurts out, "Damn, this guy is a control freak." After which Sheri realizes Brian is just doing his job and whatever it is, it's always done with a yes.

Sheridan parks the car and makes his way along the sidewalk where tiny stones are now being crushed beneath the leather soles of his shoes. As the sound is heard reverberating from the authoritative walls he now walks through the entryway where his footsteps now echo throughout the corridor. Once at the elevator this man dressed in black waits patiently for its arrival. As the minutes pass Sheri couldn't help thinking, "I wish getting to heaven was this easy." The door opens and he steps onto the carpeted floor then presses the button for the second floor and within thirty- seconds the ride is over.

As Sheri walks the remaining twenty feet to O'Daly's office he remembers a similar occasion when he had been called to this very office only to be notified that he had been transferred. Would this follow the same pattern? His presence now interrupts the light coming from the outer office, at which point an inquiring voice asks, "Sheri is that you?"

Sheri replies, "Yes Brian, please finish what you were doing, I'll keep busy."

Now comfortably seated Sheri begins reading The Theological Quarterly Review, within minutes his attention is drawn to the odor of a beeswax candle that's positioned alongside a marble display depicting a brilliant sunrise along with a portrayal of the ascension of Christ. A brass plaque beneath this work reads, "The Son shines on all of us."

Farmworth walks into the room, acknowledges Sheridan, and goes about his business. Sheri can't help but notice an uncommon degree of stress displayed on Brian's face.

Then Farmsworth voice breaks into a matter of fact tone, as he says, "It's nice to see you're on time, we'll need a few more minutes. The Bishop is concluding a meeting with the O`Sullivan brothers, they've been awarded the contract to do the needed repairs at the hospital."

Brian then disappears in the direction of O'Daly's office, leaving Sheri alone and surprised that there's such a sense of urgency. Then he notices two garment bags, and one large suitcase situated alongside of Brian's desk, all monogrammed with the Bishop's initials. A red flag begins to fly leaving Sheri to wonder if he's to be under Farmsworth's authority in O'Daly's absence.

The clock hanging on the wall directly behind, and above Farmsworth's desk reads six thirty, and with it being nearly nine hours since his last meal Sheri is beginning to experience hunger pangs. Then laughter coming from O'Daly's office breaks the silence. Now Farmsworth, O'Daly, the two O`Sullivan brothers and Stephen Chance, facility director for the diocese, can be seen making their way to the outer office, better known as the common room. With dialogue still being exchanged, all five men walk pass Sheridan and continue on into the hallway where closure finally comes to their meeting. With the O'Sullivans and Chance leaving through the corridor Farmsworth and O'Daly reenter the room. John now walks over to where Sheri is seated, and apologizes for the delay, saying, "I'm sorry things took so long." At which point the Bishop extends his hand in friendship. As both men sit down Brian continues with his duties in O'Daly's office where he gathers the blueprints, and the other documents.

O'Daly resumes the conversation by saying, "When I heard your footsteps outside the window I knew the meeting with the O`Sullivan brothers had taken too long. You know Sheri, out of all my priests, you're the only one I can recognize by his walk. The rest of them seem to sneak up on me, and before I know it I'm in a corner." Pausing for a brief moment O'Daly then continues, "That's it, I'll require everyone to wear leather- soled shoes." Both laugh thereby relieving the stress that each man had experienced that day, now sitting in agreeable silence they allow the aromatic scent of beeswax to calm their tired spirits.

Then Sheri asks, "Bishop, is something bothering you?"

Now with each man reasonably comfortable O'Daly replies, "No, not really, it's been an exhausting day, I'm quite alright. Listen Brian had intended we meet here over supper. I'll leave it up to you, cold cuts and instant soup or my brother's restaurant downtown?" A calculated response isn't needed the expression on Sheri's face says it all. Now with a satisfied response O'Daly withdraws to his office and makes the reservations.

9

Sheri is alone in the presence of the shrine again and realizes the decision he made to become a hospital chaplain ten years ago had been an excellent choice, this eight to five business wasn't his style. Although his attendance at hospital meetings was required they lacked the intensity that had been displayed here. This would certainly explain the stress on Brian's face being second in command and having the responsibility going with it would take a toll on anyone. At least Sheri had the satisfaction of seeing peace in the eyes of those he ministered to.

Still retaining an interest in the magazine Sheri continues by reading an article entitled, <u>Lost Souls, Could We Have Saved Them?</u> Very intriguing he thinks. An orientation on saving soul's using applied science, all theory, where does the real world come? This aspect of his vocation he felt uncomfortable with, having to deal with scholars who had their heads in the clouds. Maybe they should come down to earth where they could make a difference. Coming face to face with a challenge or two never hurt anyone. This really bothers Sheri for he always felt where lost souls were concerned something had blocked the message, and the only soles he ever wanted to lose were those on the bottom of his shoes!

Sheri dismisses the article and returns the magazine to the table when he notices John and Brian approaching the outer office. Brian immediately reaches for the bags and proceeds in the direction of the parking garage where he'll load the luggage into O'Daly's car and then drive it to the front of the building. Meanwhile John walks over to the perpetual display and extinguishes the candle saying, "I had this shrine commissioned hoping people would see the light, but they're too busy to catch a few rays from this Son. Oh well there's one code we all have to live by and that's the fire code, all candles are to be out if the building is unattended." O'Daly then takes one more look at the display, and says, "You know He has a fire code too."

O'Daly and Sheri now leave the office and begin walking in the direction of the elevator, where Sheri presses the button. The door opens, and both men enter, then as they make their descent O'Daly looks at the directory that's hanging on the wall, and says, "My successor will have his name here someday, and mine will be in the history books." Sheri begins to wonder if the responsibilities O'Daly is burden with has anything to do with the way he's carrying himself.

As they leave the building both men adjust to a new stride, they're now enveloped in fresh air and the odor of blossoms. Brian is now waiting at the main entrance with the sedans' engine running and points to his watch indicating they're running behind time. O'Daly hurries Sheri along, and within minutes all three men are en route to the restaurant. The

11

twenty-minute ride through downtown traffic gives O'Daly ample time to catch up on administrative matters, including the hospital progress report that was due in January. Sheri seems puzzled by the question and then says, "The report was finished on time, and was delivered by the diocesan courier to your office on the second of January." Silence now airs throughout the car leaving O'Daly's opponent at a disadvantage, that was his style and for the most part he felt it worked.

Within minutes Farmsworth breaks that silence saying, "Bishop that report was sent to the planning and development office."

Sheri begins wondering what all the fuss is about, Farmsworth knew where the report was all O'Daly had to do was ask him. Sheri begins to feel he's been left out of the picture, and worries O'Daly may have something up his sleeve. This man hadn't reached this point in his career by following others, he always exhibited strong leadership skills, and with the help of eyes and ears all over the state he's well informed.

The trio arrives at O'Daly's Corner of Ireland, around seven fifteen, it's a modest establishment, but well patronized. John's brother Timothy greets the three men at the door and then escorts them to a remote area of the dining room reserved for occasions as this. Then both men exchange glances as if to say, we'll talk later. With the waiter at hand John proceeds to order three stuffed tenderloin dinners, the choice isn't questioned the restaurant has a favorable reputation for this blue ribbon delicacy. Sheri sits in anticipation, knowing he would have to file tonight's fare under "s" for superb. Farmsworth on the other hand waits in his typical fashion, scanning the tables at the far end of the room, a real busybody. Quite an embarrassment, leaving an impression he's watching a tennis match, glancing from one table to another, and he's not even aware he's doing it.

This distraction soon comes to an end as O'Daly says, "Gentlemen you're ignoring the purpose of this dinner. We have to wrap up this matter tonight, or at best establish the ground rules you'll be playing by." Both men look at one another showing their fear of the unknown. Farmsworth begins to roll his napkin while displaying involuntary facial contractions, a pure giveaway of his uncertainty. Sheri on the other hand is as tense as a coiled spring with his external signs being well hidden. This particular trait was acquired while working with the sick, grace under fire if you will. However this business of establishing ground rules had to be defined! Just as that process was to begin two waiters arrive and carefully arrange each dinner before its intended recipient.

The following hour produces little more than sundry conversation, with each man talking about their daily routine, safe dialogue that fills those gaps between courses. With the meal now over and no one expressing a desire for dessert everyone sits around the table drinking coffee, and moving as little as possible.

With his guest somewhat more receptive O'Daly says, "Well boy's its time we get down to business." Sheri and Brian sit upright in a more formal manner as O'Daly continues, "I'm going to need your full cooperation in this matter." Sheri's concentration is broken as he recalls the last time he was a party to a discussion like this. That's when he had to fill a vacancy at a mission parish which lasted for nearly two years, not to mention having to deal with a bull moose at the entrance to the church. O'Daly's voice is getting louder, "Do I have everyone's attention? As I was trying to say I'm leaving for Rome tomorrow morning, and will be doing so without Brian." As providence would have it John's personal pager now sounds. As he glances at the telephone number O'Daly displays a sense of wonder, then excuses himself from the table and begins walking in the direction of Timothy's office.

Sheri casually looks in Brian's direction anticipating an emotional outburst, within seconds the predictability of the moment is satisfied with Farmsworth saying, "What's the old man up to now, he's well aware of my affection for Rome." Sheri is beginning to think the only thing Brian is sorry about is missing out on a paid vacation. Farmsworth continues to display his disappointment by saying, "Somebody has to keep a close eye on his itinerary otherwise O'Daly will end up in Timbuktu!"

Sheri roars with laughter then a subtle smile emerges on Farmsworth's face and he too joins in. Sheri feels this would- be the perfect opportunity to express his own concern for never making the trip to Rome and says, "I know you're disappointed Brian but it's not the end of the world. They'll be another chance in six months, and who knows maybe we'll be able to make the trip together."

Farmsworth's concedes to Sheri's reasoning however he's able to get the last word in, saying, "You maybe right, but that doesn't change the way I feel about the man. In the fifteen years I've worked for him I've never felt comfortable in my ability to predict what he'll do next, and after today I see no reason to change my mind."

Sheri wants to put closure to the matter, and says, "Well Brian that's what life's all about, change, and the impact it has on all of us."

With both men more relaxed they wait in anticipation as to the next turn of events. O'Daly can now be seen advancing in their direction, out of breath and with a hurried tone in his voice he says, "That call was from Father Murphy saying they've taken Bishop O`Rourke to Guardian Angel's Hospital where he's been stabilized."

Sheri and Brian express their concern as to the seriousness of the condition then all three men reseat themselves to the table. A waiter walks over and pours more coffee while John resumes the dialogue, saying, "It seems he was running a high fever accompanied by abdominal pain. So they rushed him to the hospital where Patrick's physician reassured everyone it wasn't serious however he did say it was in Patrick's best interest if he stayed home for a few weeks."

O`Rourke and O'Daly planned to meet each other at the J.F.K. International Airport and then they would continue their journey to Rome, now with other arrangements having to be made Brian clings to the idea he may still go. However O'Daly has other plans and says, "I'll be traveling with Patrick's assistant, and now let's continue with our business. Brian, starting tomorrow you're to familiarize Tom Waters with your duties, and do it as quickly as possible, you'll only have a few days to accomplish this task, so please don't let me down." With O'Daly retaining Brian's attention Sheri recalls Waters as an underclassman studying at the same seminary that he and Farmsworth had attended. Tom was an attentive man and would make a fast study. O'Daly concludes by saying, "Then at the appropriate time you'll be given further instructions." O'Daly's last words begin to bother Sheri, he's heard them before and now he begins to wonder where all this secrecy will lead.

Then O'Daly looks over at Sheridan and says, "You'll return to the hospital and continue with your daily routine until you're informed otherwise, and remember I expect everyone's cooperation."

Then John addresses Farmsworth's questioning mind by saying, "Brian, in the meantime you're to head back to the office and gather the progress reports for the hospital and the plans for the new children's clinic, and place them on the rear seat of the car. That way I'll be assured everything has been packed away for the trip." With O'Daly now confident his instructions had been understood he walks over to the cashier.

Brian now stands alongside of O'Daly as he pays the bill leaving Sheri alone and somewhat impressed. Now for the first time in twenty years there seems to be some kind of action, and it isn't bingo or a potluck dinner. Then he thinks all he'll need now is a mackintosh, and a little foreign intrigue. Sheridan's smile is a sure giveaway because O'Daly's voice can be heard in the distance saying, "Sheri, stop day dreaming!" He hurries in an attempt to catch up and finds both men parting company with John turning to him, saying, "You might as well follow me. Brian has taken the car and there's a forty-minute walk back to the office." Both laugh as they begin their journey.

Five minutes into their walk John brings up the topic of Sheri's manuscript, saying, "The last time we discussed this project I sensed you were experiencing some difficulty, how did things turnout?"

Sheri finally realizes O'Daly is displaying an honest interest in what he does and then replies, "I've completed the manuscript, however the editing process is another thing altogether."

Both men continue walking in silence then O'Daly asks, "What kind of research were you able to put together, you know the kind of material that can be substantiated by other publications?"

Sheri slows his stride then answers the question, "There's an expanded index with many classical references, all of which by design presents an extremely sound hypothesis."

John picks up the pace and then says, "What you're trying to tell me it's a rehash of an old story."

Sheridan is protective of the research he's been involved in and searches for a reply.

O'Daly knows what has to be said, and does so in a constructive manner, saying, "I understand this kind of undertaking is rough and at times frustrating, however there's no need to create a disappointment for yourself. This is what I want you to do, shelve your project, then complete the assignment I've given you, who knows maybe they'll be something you can use."

Sheri offers an agreeable smile then the two men walk the remainder of the way occupying themselves with memories of simpler times when life was less complicated. O'Daly then recalls his assignments as a parish priest and how each day would roll over to another allowing for more meaningful events to take place, such as Baptisms, Confirmations, and of course Matrimony. He had an opportunity to know the families, and to help them in anyway he could to achieve their goals. As the journey now comes to an end each man realizes he's found satisfaction in helping others.

As the two men turn off Amsterdam Boulevard onto St. Peter's Street they enter the diocesan parking lot. There under a single security light stands Sheri's Camero looking as it once did while on the showroom floor in 1964. Approaching the car O'Daly finishes the briefing by saying, "Sheri I'm aware this evening was less than informative. All I can say at this time is we're dealing with one of our older priest and the condition of his health. We have no idea what's wrong with him or how he ended up this way. You're to piece things together, and if a picture emerges demonstrate how that pattern had developed. All of this will be clearly defined within a day or so." With Sheri having to leave each man says goodnight.

With a turn of the ignition key and a quick look over his left shoulder Sheri begins heading home, and with any kind of luck he'll be back by eleven o'clock to relieve Father Norse in Intensive Care. Both men expressed a desire for that location due to its high- risk environment. Sheri shifts into third gear and merges back onto the interstate system where he now has a westerly heading. After a few miles Sheri realizes this was a perfect night for driving, especially with the engine ingesting the cool evening air, and the carburetor adjusting to the right mixture. With the rpm's holding steady, this Detroit Wonder has found its sweet spot, and with music from the fifty's rolling off the CD, both man and his machine seem quite content.

.

For reasons unknown a returning trip seems to take far less time than actually going somewhere and this journey confirms that observation. Maybe enjoying ones own company and being satisfied with life has something to do with the experience.

It's a little after eleven as Sheri finally reaches his destination, and all he needs to do now is register back on duty with security then relieve Father Norse. Later in the privacy of his quarters Sheri takes a beer from a small convenience refrigerator and reclines in his chair. Then he reviews the events of that evening and comes to only one conclusion he and Brian would know more in a day or so and whatever they'll be doing will have an underlying importance, all of which is vague at best. Then in a state of exhaustion he performs his duties and falls asleep.

Chapter Two

Hours later a new day arrives pushing away a haze of darkness revealing familiar images for all to recognize. As Sheri awakens he realizes the events of last evening were real and accepts the assignment as Divine Providence. He then makes preparations for the day, and within a few hours most of those duties have been completed as part of his routine. Sheri then remembers O'Daly's suggestion that he shelve the manuscript, turning around he grabs the bound pages and places them inside an envelope, then rushes in the direction of Out Patient Services. As Sheri passes through the doorway he recognizes Father Burtrom Burns sitting in a wheelchair, and asks, "Father Burns may I speak with you?"

The attendant who's been accompanying Burtrom stops, and turns the wheelchair in Sheri's direction then Burns says, "You have the advantage, do I know you?"

Sheri notices Burtrom's weakened voice and pale complexion, all indicating he's suffering from a serious illness. Sheridan hesitates, collects his thoughts, and deciding a more compassionate tone would-be needed, then says, "Yes Father, its David Sheridan. Twenty five years ago Brian Farmsworth and I helped out by moving records and materials from St. Paul's Parish while on weekend leave from the seminary."

Burtrom's voice is barely audible as he replies, "Yes, I remember now, I see by your collar you've been ordained, good I knew you would make it. Tell me Father, the other chap Putt-Putt, what ever happened to him?" That was a nickname Burtrom gave Farmsworth, you see in the evenings after records were catalogued and boxed these two would head out to play round after round of miniature golf. If anyone asked where they were off to the standard reply was, tilting at windmills.

Sheri acknowledges the inquiry by saying, "Brian never made the golf tour he was ordained as well, and presently is assistant to Bishop O'Daly. Sheri notices Burns was next in line at patient registration and decides the conversation would have to continue at another time, saying, "The nurse is looking for your paper work Father. Could we----."

In mid sentence Burtrom interrupts and completes Sheri's thoughts, "Yes, that would work out fine. I'll telephone you, I see by your hospital ID badge that you're the chaplain here."

Sheri is quick to reply, "Yes Father, and all you'll need to do is call the switchboard, they'll patch the call into my residence, or page me." All three men exchange pleasantries then express regret for such a short visit. Sheri then excuses himself and walks down the hallway in the direction of Richard Post's office, where he hands the manuscript over to the secretary for safekeeping.

Sheri picks up the pace while walking in the direction of the cafeteria, once there he settles down and begins eating breakfast. Later as Sheri is about to finish his meal Richard Post approaches the table and Sheri welcomes the chief of security saying, "Richard there's plenty of room, pull up a chair and join me." Dick has been referred to as the mountain, the sheer size of the man, six feet eight inches tall and two hundred eighty pounds would intimidate anyone. However he's a gentle courteous person as displayed here, "Thank you Father, I had intended to stop by your office this morning, now I can save the trip."

Sheri begins to wonder if there's an issue regarding the manuscript, and the way it was handled. With these thoughts still racing through his mind he asks, "How can I be of help?"

"Well Father, I heard through the grapevine you'll be on sabbatical, and was wondering if you were about to finish your internship?"

Sheri chuckles, "No, by all means no, I'm quite content curing the illnesses that plague men's souls."

Richard smiles then says, "I sure hope this rumor isn't true, you're the best thing that's happened to this hospital. In any event it would take a pretty big man to fill your shoes." Sheri is still trying to assimilate the news, however he allows Richard to continue the conversation, then Richard politely excuses himself from the table and walks away.

Sheri sits alone now and enjoys the warmth coming from the morning sunlight that's shining through a nearby window. It's been a cold endless winter with much snow, and now to be out and about without a coat and overshoes is surely a treat. He begins to think that freedom of movement meant less restraint. Meditating on this revelation Sheri wonders if this would apply to his station in life. He realizes every time life begins to stagnate there's usually a foul odor of discontentment, accompanied by discomfort, he couldn't let this happen.

The noise of drinking glasses being cleared from the tables startles Sheri, and he now knows he's running behind schedule, and leaves the cafeteria for his quarters. All the while reflecting on what Richard had said, and wonders if a schedule should be drafted for his replacement. He's barely inside the room when the telephone rings, lifting the handset he says, "Hello, Father Sheridan speaking."

"Good morning Sheri, It's Brian, I drove the Bishop to the airport this morning, and when I returned two men were familiarizing themselves with our files, along with the computer system. When I questioned them I received a short authoritative response."

Sheri asks, "Brian, was the candle extinguished when you left the office this morning?"

Farmsworth replies, "Yes, and when I returned it was burning, that's strange. What do you suppose is going on?"

Sheri continues by saying, "Listen, they're respecting tradition, especially this one, and for whatever reason, they have a purpose in whatever they're doing."

Farmsworth response is quite predictable, "I suppose, however in the future I'd like to know what's going on."

Sheri needs to pursue the conversation further and asks, "Listen, while I was finishing breakfast this morning Richard Post came over to my table saying he heard I was leaving. Would you know anything about that?"

Brian replies, "I haven't heard a thing, you'll have to take your own advice now and trust someone knows what he's doing. By the way I've forgot to mention the files pertaining to St. Paul's Parish have been flagged, and they'll be coming out of storage."

Sheri then asks, "Is that significant?"

Brian is still somewhat intimidated by the turn of events that have taken place that morning and replies, "Yes it is. However what's really strange is these guys are requesting that the diocesan courier deliver the files to the chief of security at St. Jonathan's. Look Sheri I'll have to wrap up our conversation these people are ready to leave." Brian terminates the call thereby allowing the two visitors to conclude their business. Once again the two men seek reassurance that a courier will indeed make the delivery.

Sheri begins making preparations for a replacement, there's little time, an itinerary would -be needed, and a notice posted, and then circulated to all departments. Just then a knock comes from the door, and a voice is heard saying, "Father, its Mary Ann, would you have a minute?"

Sheri opens the door and says, "Please come in, this is a pleasant surprise."

The nurse then explains, "I'm on break, and was wondering if you might help me figure out why I'm so unhappy?"

Sheri accepts the challenge saying, "Certainly, if I can."

The nurse appears a little distraught as she continues, "I've been feeling emotionally numb these days and was hoping you might understand what I'm going through."

Sheri takes a minute then says, "It could be the contentment you've been seeking for your family is too much, and you haven't been paying enough attention to yourself."

Mary Ann is in awe as she replies, "You know there maybe something to that I've been so wrapped up with everyone else I've neglected my own needs, which makes me less effective in other areas, thanks Father."

Sheri responds with a smile, and then escorts Mary Ann to the Nurse's Station, after which he returns to the office where he resumes drafting the schedule. After sometime he begins reflecting on Mary's Ann's conflict, and wonders if he's experiencing the odor of discontentment. Then he realizes man must first confront himself through involvement and then develop the courage of his own conviction. This is very unsettling for Sheri for he thought he was involved in life, however if he was honest with himself he was going through the motions. Now for the first time in years he feels challenged, and hopes by focussing on a personal inventory it would reveal those hidden talents that would afford him an opportunity to make a larger contribution to those individuals who needed it the most.

Later that morning rumors continue to circulate as to Sheri leaving the hospital, so he deals with this idle gossip by visiting the patient hoping it would distract him. Then the pager attached to his belt begins to vibrate, looking at the display, he recognizes the number as that belonging to the security unit. With only one floor between them he decides to take the staircase.

Within minutes he's standing inside the outer office waiting to be recognized. Looking across the room he notices Richard positioned in the doorway of his office motioning that he's to enter. Once inside Post closes the door and says, "Please be seated, I just received a telephone call instructing me to arrange a meeting in this office tomorrow morning at ten o' clock. Those in attendance will be yourself, Brian Farmsworth and of course me."

Sheri interrupts the briefing saying, "Richard, from whom are you getting your instructions from?"

Richard sits behind his mahogany desk as he replies, "The instructions came from an administrative assistant appointed by John O'Daly. However the orders were hand delivered this morning and will be opened at tomorrow's meeting."

Sheri then sighs in acceptance, saying, "I guess there's nothing more to do, but wait."

Richard concludes their conversation by telling Sheri of his own set of instruction which were to assist, and be at his and Brian's disposal as situations developed. With his obligation met the chief of security thanks Sheri, and with the meeting over each man parts company, Post to telephone Farmsworth, and Sheri to complete his visitation of the sick.

Sheridan is concerned that things are about to unfold and decides to telephone Farmsworth around four o'clock that afternoon saying, "Hello Brian, Richard Post informed me today of the scheduled briefing set for tomorrow morning at ten o'clock."

Farmsworth displays a frustrated tone as he replies, "I'm to travel an hour for this meeting, eat lunch, and then drive another hour back here. I'll have to arrange my entire day around this, not to mention the backlog I'll be facing when I return. Tom Waters can't be expected to resolve protocol issues alone, that comes from experience."

Sheri needs to rein Brian in and veers the topic of discussion in another direction saying, "How about a little tennis in the afternoon?"

Farmsworth then replies, "It's alright by me as long as you're the one picking up the tab." Sheri laughs and then makes arrangements to meet Brian the next morning in the cafeteria at nine-thirty, then to Dick's office for their ten o'clock meeting.

The remaining afternoon and early evening are uneventful, although while taking an excursion in the park directly across the street from the chapel that evening a young man feeding ducks abruptly confides to Sheri about his struggle with alcohol. This auto mechanic, and father of two girls sees himself as a moral failure. Knowing alcoholism as an insidious disease Sheri counsels William Case to seek out professional guidance, and then encourages William to telephone him if he ever needed a sounding board. They exchange telephone numbers, whereby allowing each to go there separate ways.

With William on his way Sheri begins to feel inadequate and frustrated. Tangible results were more gratifying he thought, then looking upward at the heavens the first evening star appears reminding him of a children's rhyme he hadn't thought of in years. Only if life were that easy he thinks. Tired and void of any emotion Sheri now agonizes over his role in making a difference in the world while improving the lives of its inhabitant's. Without a clue in what direction to take he's reminded of a saying his philosophy professor once used, "When in doubt, don't deal God out."

Chapter Three

By 6:45 a.m. the following morning a cool breeze begins rustling through the partially open privacy blinds covering the window. Tiny droplets of water fall on Sheri's face casually awaking him from an undisturbed sleep. He hears a cheep coming from a young robin singing outside his window. Then an unscheduled knock comes from the door, with no response a security officer is heard saying, "Father are you up?" Sheri grabs his bathrobe off the chair and answers the call. Looking at one another the officer exclaims, "Father you're needed at once in the Emergency Room." Excusing himself Sheri dresses and is in the ER within minutes. Once there he's guided to a room where a man is being kept alive on life support. The priest inquires as to the circumstances surrounding the incident, and is told two co-workers at an all night truck and service center had been involved in a fight, this being the result. He then asks the ambulance driver the identity of the man, and is told the authorities were presently at the scene, investigating. All of which led the attending physician to notice the man had been wearing a religious medal, indicating with probability that he was Catholic, and requested security to summon the Chaplain. Within minutes the patient is stabilized enough to allow the priest to administer the Last Rites. Upon completion of the Rite Sheri enters the staff lounge and begins pouring himself a cup of coffee. Distraught over the ER incident Sheri over fills the cup onto his hand, and is heard to say, "Damn it!"

Mary Ann sits at a nearby table and offers Sheri a napkin along with a little advise, saying, "Father that's not like you, please be more careful, we don't need you in the Burn Unit."

After Sheri is seated he places his cup down and says to the nurse, "It looks like the tables have turned and I'm the one whose lost his direction. It's so damn hard dealing with the dark side of human nature."

Mary responds in a confident manner saying, "That's why society needs both our vocation's while dealing with the darker side of man. I know it's not an easy thing to do, but somebody has to take the responsibility." Seeing Sheri hadn't an opportunity to freshen up that morning the nurse says, "Look

Father, you haven't shaved, and the sounds coming from your stomach tells me you haven't eaten breakfast either. Please take better care of yourself." Sheri is feeling more comfortable now and returns to his quarters.

After Sheri had shaven both he and his reflection can be seen walking down the highly polished floor toward the cafeteria. By 9:30 he's finished breakfast, and cultivated a better perspective toward the ER crisis and begins to feel the thought process or a lack there of was the catalyst for most action. He then recalls its origin in the Biblical account of Cain and Able then comes to the conclusion that he shouldn't be surprised with human nature being what it was. Completing that thought he notices Farmsworth about to be seated and abandons the mental exercise as Brian says, "While in line I overheard people talking about an accident case where a chaplain was called in for Last Rites. Sounds serious." Sheri gives an accounting of the incident, at which point Farmsworth's complexion draws pale as he voices his personal concerns, "David you're the better man, we're not cut from the same cloth. Each of us has different talents, and you seem comfortable here as chaplain, as for myself the bureaucracy of the Church has been my life." After all these years each man seems to have found a special niche where everyone benefits.

Sheri glances at the wall clock and says, "It's already 9.50, we had better pick up the pace otherwise Post will page us over the intercom, and we can do without that embarrassment."

As both men patiently wait at the front counter Sally Leland the office secretary approaches the pair and escorts them into Richard's office, where he's heard saying, "Thank you Sally. Gentlemen, before we get started it must be understood everything we discuss now and in the future must be held in complete confidence!"

Then Richard takes a key from his shirt pocket and unlocks the center drawer to his deck and produces two envelopes. One marked Instructions, and the other Warehouse Inventory. With a quick release of a hand-carved letter opener the first document is retrieved. Richard quietly begins reviewing the contents. Brian and Sheri now wait patiently for their directives. The paper from which the instructions are to be read bears the Bishop's seal, making the chief of security feeling at best foreign in this matter. Post continues with the task at hand and begins to read aloud.

Good morning Gentlemen:

"I would like to take this opportunity to express my gratitude to Richard for participating as mediator in this endeavor, and with that being said we'll address the matter at hand. Brian Farmsworth you're to immediately relieve David Sheridan as chaplain at St. Jonathan's Hospital. Upon satisfactory completion of this project, you'll be reassigned to your diocesan duties. Your personal property will be at your disposal only by request and that's to be made through Richard's office. If need arises to assist David Sheridan it'll be done by his request only, at which point you're to inform Richard of the urgency and he'll make the arrangements for someone to cover your duty assignment. Finally, when your expertise are required outside the hospital you're to abandon all garments identifying you as a priest and join Sheridan in civilian attire, and while operating in this capacity you're to make no reference to the Church, it's vocation, or attitudes while dealing with others."

"David Sheridan, you'll have a full twenty-four hours from now to place whatever personal effects that aren't needed into the care of Richard Post, then you'll familiarize Brian with the schedules, routines, and obligations of the Chaplain's Office. While on this assignment you're to wear only casual clothing, and you're to inform no one as to the purpose of this exercise, if a situation does arise it'll be handled on a need to know basis!"

"With regards to your departure and destination, that'll take place tomorrow at 1 p.m., you're to travel East to Albany, and Northwest to Route 28. Proceed through the Pine Tree Community, then just opposite the information booth turn left on Portage Road and drive 3/10th of a mile and turn right into the parking lot. This is your destination, Birch Lodge, from here you're to relieve Adam White companion and guardian to Father Burns. Adam will instruct you as to Burtrom's convalescence care and medical needs and will be your relief for days off and errands. Sheri, Burns is a devoted priest, however there's been something holding this man down for decades, and before his condition worsens I want to make sure he's comfortable in body and spirit. In order for that to happen you'll have to look into this matter on my behalf, with that said I must caution against infringements of any kind. If a situation arises that requires clarification you'll immediately inform Richard of the uncertainty, and he'll supply a response either from himself or another who's in authority."

"In conclusion the standard response to all inquiries as to Father Sheridan's whereabouts will be, he's temporarily assigned to the Bishop's Instate Missionary Program. This directive is to take effect at 7 o'clock tomorrow morning, and as always I'm sure each of you will give this your full attention."

Sincerely
John J. O'Daly

With a sense of achievement Richard leans back in his chair and returns the letter to it's envelope. The only sound now being heard is that of Brian tapping the arm of his chair. Then, without warning he blurts out, "That's what this is all about, making an old man comfortable. Rearranging the lives of everyone, when all he needs is a shrink." Sheri is clearly agitated and gives Brian a scornful look, then glances in Richard's direction. Dick now feels its necessary to step in, and he says, "Like it or not O'Daly's the boss, and from where I'm sitting there's no better time than now to get the ball rolling. The instructions are clear, if an emergency presents itself you're to telephone my office, or after hours page me at this number." Richard hands each man his business card then the telephone rings and he finishes the conversation by saying, "Will you fellows excuse me, I'll contact each of you later today."

Sheri walks through the doorway wondering what he's to expect next, and is reminded of his last wilderness experience, which left him isolated and bored. If there's a silver lining to this cloud he'd better find it fast.

Sheri then catches up with Brian, who expresses his disappointment by saying, "This is a prime example of getting a curve thrown at you. If I weren't cognizant of O'Daly's abilities, I'd chalk this up to an elaborate script for a B-Rated Movie. Oh well, what's next on the agenda, hosting a women's auxiliary tea? Maybe a rummage sale or MC a chicken a la king awards dinner. That's it, I'm over the edge, I'm out of here!"

As the weather conditions begin to clear Sheri suggests they walk outside and make plans for the transition. They enter the visitor's garden where Sheri voices his frustration, "I'm upset with you and your attitude, those comments regarding Burns, and him needing a shrink were uncalled for. You're the most selfish son of a bitch I've seen in a long time!"

Farmsworth voices an angry tone saying, "See here Sheri, I'm trained not only as a priest, but as a bureaucrat, I could possibly do more harm than good as a chaplain. O'Daly's directives are out of perspective with the spiritual needs of the patients!"

Sheri is baffled with Brian's logic and replies, "You might be on to something."

Brian stands there in awe and then says, "I'd like to understand this, you're wrong and I'm right, that's a switch."

For nearly twenty five years these two men rarely saw eye to eye on anything and when an occurrence did take place it was done out of political necessity. That is until now when Sheri affirms his position saying, "An hour ago I wouldn't have given a tinker's damn what you thought. However, under the present circumstances there's only one inescapable conclusion, neither of us feels comfortable navigating in uncharted waters."

Brian sees an opportunity to bolster his self-esteem, and defines a tentative plan, saying, "We're ducks out of water on this one, it seems ignorance is breeding fear with neither of us knowing what to expect perhaps the best thing we can do is confront the beast head on. You'll have to rely on Post and myself being available. That's easy enough, we're a telephone call away. That should work until we have a better understanding of the situation." With that said both men now walk along the wet pathway and through the evaporating mist that's coming from the heated pavement, and make their way back to the hospital lobby.

Most of the afternoon is spent reviewing an itinerary Sheri had prepared, with the exception of a coffee break it was all business. Just as they are concluding the briefing, Sheri's telephone rings. It's Richard Post, advising him that the accommodations for Farmsworth would -be Room 312 on the third floor. This room is presently unoccupied, and is usually reserved for family members who had to travel great distances.

Richard continues the conversation by asking, "Seeing I have your attention while you were in the ER this morning did you get the name of the individual you administered the Last Rites to?" Sheri responds, "You're asking the impossible, between the bandages and the activity surrounding his care I was focusing on the Rite, and getting out of the way. Why are you asking?"

Richard's response is quick and to the point, "Your telephone number was among his personal effects. There's a detective here in my office, and would like to ask you a few questions. It'll only take a few minutes, you better come on down and get this matter cleared up."

Sheri instinctively knows the man Post was referring to was William Case. Now an air of urgency fills the room as Sheri begins explaining the situation to Brian, "That was Richard, he wants me in his office as soon as possible. A detective is asking question about the ER episode this morning and needs a few answers." Farmsworth looks puzzled as the events begin to unfold and listens as Sheri continues, "There is something you can do for me. Track down the whereabouts of a young man by the name of Case, he was admitted this morning, and probably taken directly from the ER into Surgery and then to Intensive - Care."

Farmsworth struggles with his sense of direction and replies, "Where are these places?" Midway through the doorway Sheri turns around and says, "In the manila folder, there's a diagram of the entire facility. It's self-explanatory. When you're finished, we'll meet outside of Richard's office."

As Sheri rushes down the hallway he can't help but wonder what set of circumstances led to this altercation. Opening the plate glass door he passes into the receiving room and sees Richard along with detective Brad Shimner both anxiously awaiting his arrival. All three exchange pleasantries and immediately walk into Richard office whereupon Post closes the door and says, "Please be seated gentlemen. As you know Father a patient was admitted this morning and you're the one who administered the Last Rites to that person." Sheri agrees in silence as Richard continues, "This man had in his possession a piece of paper with a telephone number written on it. A check with the telephone company records reveals that number to be yours, that's why Sergeant Shimner requested that you stop by."

As silence fills the room Shimner asks, "Tell me Father, do you know how this paper came to be in William Case's possession?"

With nothing to hide and feeling very uncomfortable Sheri replies, "Last evening around 7 o'clock while I was walking in Felmore Park our paths crossed. I was sitting on a bench near the pond, at which point William strikes up a conversation implying he had a drinking problem, but wasn't quite sure if it had turned into alcoholism. Then he continued to speak of his life being pretty much in shambles, and how the family had been separated." With little more to offer Sheri concludes by saying, "The man needed someone to talk to, and with everything having been said I gave him my telephone number in the event he needed to discuss the matter further."

The Sergeant then asks, "Father, could you tell if he had been drinking?"

Sheri is uncomfortable with the question, and replies, "Yes, if he had been drinking alcohol, however William wasn't in that condition!" Sheri secures his position by saying, "Look sergeant, the Seal of the Confessional doesn't apply here, nevertheless something's are held in confidence and this particular incident falls under that heading."

Shimner is clearly agitated, and now confronts Sheri saying, "All we're trying to do is find out what happened, if we ruffle a few feathers so be it."

Sheri knows the officer has his job to do, but also is aware of his responsibilities, and then replies in a confident manner, "If you're ruffling the feathers I'll be the one smoothing them back down again!"

Richard now realizes the situation was about to get out of control and suggests if a need did arise where Sheri had to be reached again it could be done through his office. With arrangements made Shimner leaves the two men poised for an argument. Richard feels a reprimand is in order and addresses Sheridan saying, "You know better than that, Brad was probing around in good faith, looking for facts, not excuses."

Sheri postures himself for a defense saying, "Shimner was ready to cross the line, and I wasn't going to let that happen. Furthermore, when this kid pulls through this mess he's going to need help putting the pieces back together and from where I'm sitting there's a lack of volunteers!"

Post retorts, "Look at this situation from my point of view this department isn't equipped to go around rescuing stray puppies and men!"

45

Sheri isn't about to waste his breath and says, "Everyone is entitled to an opinion, and you just spent yours!"

With the tension increasing with each passing minute both men recognize behavior like this could very well fracture their friendship. At which point Richard offers an olive branch saying, "It's getting late, we'll talk about this before you leave tomorrow." With this concluding their discussion Sheri leaves the battlefield behind, and meets Farmsworth waiting in the outer office.

Brian sees the frustration displayed in Sheri's face and asks, "What in the world was going on in there?"

Sheri smiles and then says, "The shit just hit the fan!"

Brian demands an explanation saying, "You're leaving this place and the trouble you stirred up. I'm the one staying behind dealing with the aftermath, so you better let me know what's going on!"

Sensing Brian's need for self-preservation Sheri gives in by saying, "Shimner wanted me to violate an ethical issue which may have compromised my ability to help another person."

Farmsworth then replies, "Is that all, you didn't have to argue over that."

Sheri shakes his head in amazement as they move in the direction of the cafeteria. Then from a limited selection both men familiarize themselves with the menu and then enter the dining room where their anticipation is finally satisfied.

After dinner both men walk into the visitor's garden where they sit and enjoy the silence of the evening, then Brian asks, "I'd like to know more about that breach of confidentially you mentioned earlier."

Sheri knows the same question could be asked at a later date so he replies, "I've been giving that a great deal of thought and believe it wouldn't have jeopardized much. However, of greater significance is maintaining a trust between William and myself. If that were to be violated I'm sure his faith in me would had been shattered, and an opportunity to assist him when he needed it the most, lost. You know Brian, making judgement calls is part of our business, and this happened to be one of those times. No matter what aspect of our careers we're dealing with, others will hold us to a higher standard. That's what this is all about, maintaining that standard."

With the evening turning into night Sheri directs Farmsworth to room 312 and then returns to his quarters only to contemplate his next assignment, and its possible complications.

Chapter Four

The next morning after breakfast, Sheridan and Farmsworth start hospital rounds, which includes the Intensive Care Unit where William Case has been admitted. After being informed of his critical condition, they agree that Brian would report to Sheri on his progress in the days ahead. By 10:30 am, the procedural rite of passage had begun, Sheri had already returned his I. D. pass, and keys to security. Leaving only the removal of his personal effects from his room that had been his home for all these years to the security section in the basement. Once there he realizes courage has displaced the apprehension he's been feeling and the disappointment is now being replaced with a sense of duty, and a challenge he's required to meet. Now with this new insight his spirit seems to soar with enthusiasm as he continues with the task at hand.

By 11 30 a.m. Sheri has changed into casual clothes and is rearranging the room, when he hears a knock coming from the door. Brian stands in the doorway saying, "The staff is holding a farewell luncheon for you, so gather your thoughts and bags, we'll do this thing together." Brian's tenure as a priest had been restricted to office management and now he's demonstrating compassion toward humanity. That's a switch, maybe a transformation had taken place and if so he's definitely chaplain material. As these tall slender figures advance through the corridor one couldn't help but think their seemingly diverse personalities had to of been a characteristic John O'Daly recognized as compatible if they were given an opportunity to comply with his request.

With Brian accompanying him Sheri enters the oak-paneled dining room where he's greeted by thirty or so staff members who now stand, and begin to applaud his arrival. As the two make their way to the head table, Sheri's green eyes makes contact with each person he passes. This certainly is the high point of his career, with each participant praising Sheri's contribution not only to patients, but also to the staff and their families. Each who chooses to speak has a specific memory he or she shares. All too soon the event is coming to a close with a few still milling around wishing him a final farewell. Richard Post stands at the perimeter and motions that he'd like a final word.

Finally, after ten minutes all have left, leaving Brian and Sheri bidding one another goodbye.

Sheri now walks in the direction of Richard's office when he stops in front of the hospital directory hanging midway on the wall. He had routinely past this way paying little attention to its presence, however now he realizes his name had been replaced with Brian's as designated chaplain. With his name now gone from the listing there's little to do but leave. With a few last words from Post, Sheri is able to depart through the sunlit lobby.

With a release of the competition clutch and the sound of a chirp coming from a rear tire the vintage Chevy pulls away from the hospital canopy onto Chester Street, then moments later onto Interstate 87. A mellow reverberating sound coming from the motor placing Sheri in a state of complacency, allowing him to finally sever ties with the hospital. Although he's no longer affiliated with the institution he can't help but recall the restricted contact he had with the outside community. Sheri believes this certainly had handicapped his social life, and to a greater degree will cramp Farmsworth's style as well. Could this had been O'Daly's strategy right all along, to expand their horizons?

The two and half -hour trip being only half over, David realizes that he knows nothing about Burtrom Burns, except for a few weekends spent sorting material for storage some twenty-five years ago. To make matters worse, his peers all of which are gone, leaving Sheri at a proverbial dead end. The only recent contact they've had was a brief encounter en route to Burtrom's out patient appointment. All of which leaves Sheri with the impression the old man was suffering from a serious illness or even perhaps senility. Out of frustration he forsakes the mental gymnastics in favor of dealing with situations as they are presented, putting one foot in front of the other and relying on divine providence.

With the journey almost complete Sheri makes a hard left turn onto Portage Road, the Camero now conforms to the contours of the lane, leaving 3/10th of mile to travel. In that short distance Sheri reviews a preconceived image of his destination. A four room, rustic clapboard cabin, complete with a steel smokestack protruding from a roof covered in half-lap roofing material, and making this mental excursion more difficult was the overgrown shrubbery covering the walkway. With the odometer registering 3/10th of a mile Sheri now notices a gate that had been left opened. He now shifts into second gear as he passes through the opening and immediately stops. Now with a soft cloud of dust obstructing his view Sheri just sits in amazement as the particles of dust clear from his line of vision. Situated before him lies a 300-foot well graded hardpan parking lot. The far side facing him has an elongated guardrail with steel straps attached to it's uprights, a portion of which had been sectioned out to accommodate a fieldstone walkway set in concrete which has wildflowers growing on each side. The staircase leading onto the porch use's the flat surface area of logs that had been sawn through the middle, lending themselves as treads. The porch grand as it seems is readied to proclaim the arrival of its guest. Realizing he's just sitting there, Sheri idles across the parking lot and shuts off his engine alongside a station wagon that's parked in front of this magnificent edifice.

He gets out of the car and walks along the pathway and up the staircase onto the porch. There facing him are two large hand carved oak doors. Directly midway opposite one- another two large stags are engaged in mortal combat. Sheri then confronts the two wooden beasts by grabbing the door striker and impelling the knocker against the brass plate sounding his presence. Moments later, a tall man of muscular build with shoulder length hair, apparently from the nearby Mohawk Nation answers the call. Sheri isn't prepared for what he sees. Now with the door open an enormous stone- fireplace and its twelve -foot solid bird's-eye maple mantel is seen as the centerpiece of this grand display. To the right are shelves with framed photographs of individuals, and events celebrated in yesteryears, all of which are gone with the exception being the memories that had been enshrined. Just left of the mantelpiece are animal trophies of hunts long past. Six to eight feet from the hearth, in a semicircle are four chairs and a couch crafted from birch logs and upholstered in leather. The cathedral ceiling constructed of spruce timber rises twenty-two feet from which a long chain hangs from its apex thereby supporting an exquisite chandelier, once illuminated it'll depict a forest and it's creatures. The Hardwood floors having been pegged have a high gloss expressing a fluid flow. The dimension could easily be twenty by thirty feet.

Sheri is still bathing in the grandeur of this revelation, when a voice is heard to say, "Welcome, we've been expecting your arrival."

David pauses to collect his thoughts, then acknowledges the greeting by saying, "Please forgive me, all this is so exquisite."

The Native-American closes the door and then introduces himself, "My name is Alex Hunter I'm your host, I also manage the place for Bishop O'Daly, and you've just entered one of the last vestiges of Nineteenth Century Americana. You see a wealthy industrialist by the name of Theodore Green constructed this building in 1890 and used it for hunting and family recreation, those sorts of things. Then with the passing of time the family lost interest, thereby allowing the trustees of the estate to turn the Lodge, and surrounding property over to the Church. However, they did stipulated there were to be no changes to the building or grounds and it's never to be sold. So, here we are beneficiaries of Ted's generosity."

With the men now engaged in a conversation, Adam White enters the room interrupting Alex's orientation saying, "Would you excuse us, I'm to instruct Father on Burtrom's care." Alex, already knowing the importance of Sheri's mission leaves the room to prepare supper.

Sheri offers his own observations as to Burtrom's medical condition saying, "Its obvious from the brief encounter I had with Father Burns he's suffering from neurological and physical diseases." Sheri feels a need to establish the boundaries with regards to medical diagnosis and treatment issues, then continues to say, "Although medically trained, I'm in no position to be of any real help to Burtrom. So with that said, what's his daily routine like?"

Adam replies, "Burtrom usually rises between eight and eight-thirty in the morning eats breakfast, then dinner at noon, supper around six-thirty in the evening, and is in bed around ten. As far as personal hygiene issues, he's capable of taking care of those himself. A housekeeper will come in on Monday, Tuesday, and Friday, she'll also do the laundry, you're to attend to hospital, clinic, and medication schedules." With bags in hand, Adam moves in the direction of the door, and then says, "If there's a need Alex has my number." As if in a failed performance this actor leaves the melodrama of Birch Lodge behind as he passes through the doorway.

Sheri acknowledges White's departure with a good-bye, then goes about exploring the first floor for any sign of his host. As he walks through the dining room he notices Alex preparing dinner in the kitchen. Alex had overheard Adam as he was leaving and greets his guest with a pronounced smile saying, "Welcome to our world."

Sheri displays a straight face and then replies, "Can it be fixed?" With that, both men break out laughing, and with tearing flowing Sheri tries to compose himself long enough to say, "I've never seen anything like it. In less than five minutes, Adam informed me of my duties regarding Burtrom's care then he was out the door. It was like a thunderstorm, I saw a streak of lightning then heard the thunder as the door slammed." By this time both men are bent over in laughter.

As this charged moment returns to normalcy Sheri is once again faced with trying to understand the motives behind whites behavior, and asks, "Did something happen causing Adam to respond in such a fashion?"

As Alex places that evening's dinner aside he begins to explain, "You're asking the impossible but I'll give it a try. It all started eight years ago when Burtrom began exhibiting signs of his illness along with the need for special care. The Bishop approached Adam, and with his consent made him Burtrom's guardian. Whereby allowing John to make arrangements for Father's care at several institutions, none of which fulfilled Burtrom's expectation. So, six months ago it was decided that he'd be better off right here at the Lodge, it's worked out well for Burtrom. However Adam developed cabin fever soon after they arrived. That's it in a nutshell, he couldn't wait to leave."

With the preparation for supper now completed a guided tour would -be needed to familiarize Sheri with the building, and its amenities. Walking from the kitchen through a spacious hallway adjacent to a window overlooking the rear grounds sits a bench built into the wall. Across from that, attached to a wooden rail, is a coat rack composed of deer hooves, articulated to receive garments. Walking to the other end of the hallway where it meets a passageway Alex points in the direction of the den which has been paneled in knotty pine, and meticulously polished with a beeswax compound, filling the room with a pleasant fragrance.

They leave through the rear entrance of the building and visit a small hydroelectric plant being fed by a tributary of Silver

Lake, from here the running water impels a generator, which produces electricity for the Lodge. Then walking along the water's edge Alex and Sheri pass two Adirondack Guide Boats beached on the shore, then Alex gestures in an attempt to get Sheri's attention, and says, "There, on the second floor to the right of those two windows is your room. In the evening you'll be able to sit on the balcony and watch the fish feeding by the light of the moon. Alex notices the time and continues by saying, "We better get back, Burtrom will be waking up soon."

Sheri is inquisitive as to the schedule and asks, "Is that part of a regular routine?" In a hurried state Hunter replies. "Yes, at least for the time he' s been here, and from what I can see he needs the rest, I hear all sorts of commotion coming from his room at night, all of which indicates he's suffering from some kind of sleep disorder. There's something seriously wrong."

After entering the Lodge both men return to the grandeur of the Great Room with its magnificent fireplace and décor. Alex now retrieves Sheri's bag, and continues leading the way to the staircase, and begins walking up the four-foot wide stairs to a landing and again up another six steps to the second floor, and then along a cantilevered hallway. Alex now acquaints Sheri with the surroundings of his room, then returns to the kitchen.

After Sheri is settled in he walks across the room and directly onto the balcony where he reclines in one of the two Adirondack chairs. Now with his eyes closed he recognizes the scent of pine being carried through the air, and with very little effort he dozes off.

After an hour or so Sheri realizes he had fallen asleep, and with noise now coming from the kitchen he makes his way back to the dining room where he finds Alex and Burtrom eating their supper. After preparing a plate Sheri joins the others at the table and begins speaking with Alex, which allows him an opportunity to observe Burns. At this point he's able to recognize Burtrom's withdrawn nature, which is indicative of an anxiety disorder.

With their meal now finished Alex and Sheri remain at the table while Burt returns to his room. Now with the freedom to speak Sheri says, "Burtrom is exhibiting signs of an anxiety disorder."

Alex then suggests they wash the dinner dishes and discuss the matter later that evening while relaxing on the patio.

With the kitchen now cleaned both men are able to reposition the lounge chairs on the patio, hoping to get a better view of the fading sunlight and its radiant pastel colors being reflected from the surface of the lake. The panorama now begins to unfold in a nearby marsh where two white tail deer make their way to the other side then fish seem to leap over one another in mid-air attempting to feed on the many insects that surround the water. Alex expresses a contented sigh, looks over at Sheri and then asks, "What do you think of the artwork?"

Sheri is overwhelmed with what he sees and replies, "You're putting me in an awkward position, I'm lost for words."

The proud Native -American, with generations of wisdom flowing through his veins, exemplifies his challenge by saying, "See how the doe holds her nose high in the air, she's teaching the fawn to identify scent, and recognize danger. Over there beside the large boulder is a coyote with a limp, and from that I envision he's in pain and is experiencing fear, because the animal isn't as agile as before, with him now knowing he's easy prey. I hear this valley singing with emotion, bringing adventure to every life form. The environment is only a reflection of the Great Spirit and His Creation. Here you will experience harmony."

Sheri is humbled by his lack of perception, and tries to atone, by saying, "Could it be that mankind is the real animal, and possibly the most dangerous?"

Hunter nods in agreement, and moves in the direction of a new topic of discussion, saying, "I spoke with the Bishop yesterday and he indicated a need to speak with you this evening. Throughout the conversation you were referred to as Sheri, how should I address you?"

Sheridan considers Alex as a friend and implies he's to use the short version of his last name because it sounds better and then recounts those incidents since childhood when family members and friends affectionately referred to him as Sheri because he blushed so easily. Redirecting the discussion he asks, "Did John indicate what his concerns were?"

Alex gives a reassuring reply saying, "I wouldn't worry about it, he'll probably ask if you're settled in." As the evening yields it's grandeur to the darkness Alex suggest they wait inside for O'Daly's call.

Leaving the kitchen with a coffeepot and two cups, this unlikely pair are en route to Alex's favorite room where they can sit amongst the fish, figuratively speaking, for the catch of yesteryears have been mounted and now hang from the walls. Once there, Sheri walks over and admires two trophies, a trout and a large mouth bass, then examines a display rack of fishing rods. He anxiously pours another cup of coffee, and sits in an overstuffed leather chair then stares across the room in wonder.

Alex looks through a nearby window, and exclaims, "It's eight-twenty I wonder if the circuits are busy?" They then decide to play cards, and as the game progresses each man begins to show interest in what they're doing, then the telephone rings. Alex answers the call and begins talking with O'Daly. After a few minutes he then motions for Sheri. Taking the receiver David listens to O'Daly's instructions adhering to every word, and responds in a vague manner. Sometime later O'Daly terminates the call allowing the men to resume their card game once again.

Sheri not wanting to leave anything to chance takes a minute from the game and sums up his conversation with John, saying, "He wants us to work together, if we team up there's a good chance of finding a solution to Burtrom's problems." Both men smile, for they've reached a well- defined understanding of their direction.

Alex uses the occasion to discuss Burtrom present situation, saying, "Burt's been this way for sometime, and has always been heavily medicated. I'm not sure he'll be of any help, it could take years before he comes around, I'm beginning to wonder if time will be on our side."

Sheri takes more of an optimistic approach saying, "We'll need plenty of help, and I know two people who are in a perfect position to lend a hand, they're Brian Farmsworth, and Richard Post. I've known these fellows for years, each are dedicated, and loyal men they'll be a definite asset."

Both men feel more comfortable with the situation, and now realize that the evening had past far to quickly and decide to call it a night, with Alex finally suggesting that Sheri sleeps in, in the morning.

Chapter Five

Awaking the following morning Sheri becomes acclimated to his new surroundings and then walks to a nearby window where he watches a flock of ducks skirmishing along the shoreline. Loosing interest in the birds Sheri dresses and walks downstairs to the kitchen. Pouring a cup of coffee he watches Alex returning from the lake. Alex enters the mud- room and hangs a burlap bag of corn meal on a nearby wall hook then accounts for his absence saying, "There's two mallard ducks each with a clutch, feeding them once a day makes it a little easier for the mothers." Seeing that Sheridan hadn't eaten breakfast Alex grabs a loaf of sourdough bread off the counter, saying, "A few slices of this will add a little flavor to that coffee."

Sheri covers the slice with butter then replies, "This is really exceptional."

As Sheri takes another slice Alex turns his attention to Burtrom, saying, "Burt came down for breakfast around eight-thirty, drank a cup of coffee then returned to his room. You could say he looked a little peaked."

Sheri realizes he needs to take manners in his own hands, and replies, "You may be right, the first thing that comes to mind is his liver. Something could be going on there, he'll need a full examine, with blood work, to check for liver enzymes, and a blood count wouldn't hurt either. The man is getting on in years and there could be complications with his medication. Anyway, there isn't much that can be done on a weekend except getting the ball rolling, and I'll do that by calling Farmsworth this evening. Maybe he'll be able to locate Burtrom's physician, and who knows maybe there's a chance he'd be willing to make the drive up here. I do know one thing, we have a delicate situation, and one way or another Burt will get the care he needs." With both men in agreement the remainder of the day is spent doing routine chores while giving Burtrom the needed attention he required.

Sheri is finally able to place a call into Farmsworth's office that evening. Brian seems surprised to learn what Sheridan had experienced, because O'Daly had never spoken to anyone in the office about Birch Lodge or the circumstances surrounding its existence. Farmsworth is eager to help and listens as Sheri says, "Burtrom is experiencing complications, and I feel the situation could be better managed if his doctor could make the trip up here." Brian expresses concern for Burt's welfare, and offers to do what he can, and informs Sheri to expect an update as to his progress sometime Sunday evening.

The following morning while seated at the breakfast table Alex informs Sheri that Burtrom never made his customary appearance. Alarmed by this event Sheri immediately rushes to the old man's room whereupon he finds Burt running a high fever, turning to Alex he says, "This man needs lab work done now!" Then with little discussion and much difficulty Alex and Sheri carry Burntrom downstairs and gently place the old man in the front seat of the Camero. Within minutes he's being transported to St. Jonathan's Hospital. While en route Sheri wonders if Alex has reached Brian, then looking over at Burt he finds the old man riddled in perspiration, and with no way of making him comfortable Sheri continues driving. Now sitting back in his seat Sheri feels confident everything's been done that can be, and turns his attention to the Chevy's dependability and marvels as to it's performance, all the while thinking if the situation were different the trip would-be more pleasurable.

With the trip now over Sheri shifts the Camero into second gear and redlines the tachometer as he turns onto Empire Avenue, within a few short minutes he's parked in the receiving area. At which point two attendants approach the car and delicately seat Burtrom in a wheelchair and begin wheeling their patient into a designated triage room. Physically and emotionally exhausted Sheri walks in the direction of the nurse's station, where Farmsworth intercepts him saying, "What the hell's going on, how fast were you driving? Alex telephoned a little while ago saying Burtrom had taken a turn for the worse and you decided to drive him here!"

Sheri is barely able to compose himself when he's compelled to explain the circumstances leading to their unscheduled visit, saying, "It's simple, when I spoke with you yesterday his condition was stable, then overnight things changed dramatically."

Brian now reveals the results of his inquiry into the whereabouts of Burtrom's physician, saying, "Burt's records indicate he's been a walk-in patient, being seen by a different physician on each visit.

Sheri's reaction is somewhat predictable as he's heard to say, "This is bullshit, the man's never had any regular follow-ups, how could he if he's never had a primary care physician!"

Sheri sits down and begins considering his options then he suddenly remembers Burns would need authorization if he's to be treated. Sheridan then leaves Burtrom in Brian's care enabling him to make the needed arrangements.

Sheri returns an hour later and meets Farmsworth in the waiting room where Brian suggests they both speak with the attending physician. After some delay the Doctor agrees to speak with both men saying, "Hello, I'm Doctor Keno, I understand both of you are friends of Father Burns." With the customary handshakes being exchanged Sheri eagerly seeks out Keno's diagnosis, and in return the Doctor addresses their concerns saying, "Well, Father's a very sick man, I have two concerns at this moment, an infection and the other dehydration. We've started two i. v.'s, the next twenty-four hours should tell us what's going on. By that time the lab results will be back, and we'll be able to go from there. Figure a two or three day hospital stay at the minimum." Keno's attention is now drawn to the medical charts before him, and then with a tone of urgency he excuses himself.

With Burtrom under Doctor Keno's care Brian brings up the topic of William Case, saying, "I tried visiting Mr. Case and was stopped by an officer standing at the door. I was then informed Bill was under their custody and that he wasn't able to have visitors. The whole situation seems peculiar, you'd think there would had been some kind of coverage in the newspaper. In any event I asked Richard and he was of no help. With the conversation being one-sided Brian notices Sheri's hollowed expression and realizes the man hadn't taken a day off in over a month and voices concern, "Burtrom is going to be here for at least two or three days, maybe more. And with no accommodations for your stay here you should think about trekking back to the Lodge. You need the time off, go fishing, get some rest, and when Burt's is ready to travel, I'll run him up to Birch myself. While you're at it, stop off somewhere and add a few items to your wardrobe, collegiate attire doesn't go well in timber country. Anyway, your instructions are to care for Burtrom and look into the cause of his condition, and that's being accomplished to some degree right now, so start taking care of yourself."

With a twinkle in his eye Sheri's able to see light at the end of the tunnel and realizes the situation is indeed under control whereby allowing him to give Farmsworth a back handed farewell as he leaves the building.

With a brief stop at a nearby outlet Sheri makes a few purchases, all items he thought would-be needed while staying in the Lake Region of upper New York State. Now with this task completed, and having developed a new perspective he retraces the route back through the mountains.

Around six-thirty that evening Alex notices a cloud of dust rising from the roadway, looking closer he recognizes the Camero and now walks over to where its parked and says to Sheridan, "I didn't expect seeing you for two or three days."

Sheri grabs the shopping bags from the rear seat of the car, and says, "You're looking at a new man." Alex's curiosity has now peaked, and he willingly lends a hand hoping he'll hear more. Sheri then continues to say, "Those two days you're referring to are all mine and I'm going to take full advantage of what you can offer in out-door adventure."

Alex then exclaims, "Alright, finally I've got my first convert, and you know it was worth the wait." With that said both men return to the Lodge.

While sitting at the supper table that evening Alex finally inquires as to Burtrom's condition, and with Sheri's appetite now being satisfied he replies, "Depending on the lab results Burtrom will be hospitalized at least for tomorrow or even Wednesday. Hopefully by that time we'll have a prognosis, and while all this is happening I'm under orders from Farmsworth to kick back and relax." Alex, having known Sheri only a few days already sees a change in the mans attitude, reassuring him as to the outcome of this exercise.

An hour later as the two men were sitting on the patio Sheri asks if there was a medical doctor in the area, and then is informed by Alex that Doc Middleton had an office ten miles South of Birch on route 28.

Now with some degree of enlightenment Sheri says, "I found out today Burtrom doesn't have a regular physician, and every time he's been seen at the walk-in clinic a different doctor has examined him. That's why I asked, we'll needed a primary care physician who'll stay on top of things." With an intuitive feeling of chaos ahead Sheri avoids any further discussion of Burtrom, saying, "Enough of this business, what's on the agenda for tomorrow?"

Alex begins detailing the events of the next day saying, "We'll have breakfast and leave well before Littea Milner arrives." Sheri is now curious as to the preemptive departure and inquires as to the rush. Alex now grins as he recounts the saga of Littea's matrimonial troubles, saying, "It all started some years ago when her husband John, a real naturalist, came across an infant porcupine that had been abandoned. He quickly adopted the creature and nursed it back to health. Then as time went on the two became inseparable, leaving Littea, a full blooded Mohawk with a very attractive figure I might add, feeling John had paid to much attention to the animal. So with silken material in hand she fashioned a clinging Paris Original

71

with a slit along the right side. Then one evening fully equipped to get his attention she sashayed in a seductive manner past John. Then in a very gracious manner Littea began to seat herself with the intention of exposing a little leg, when unbeknownst' to her Spike who had already taken residence in the chair implanted two dozen quills in Littea's best side. Needless to say the fabric of choice left little resistance allowing for a deep set. It was decided at that point, sorry for the pun, she would ride belly down in the back of John's pick-up to Doc Middleton's office, and some say while John drove past Buck's Roadhouse Littea could be heard cursing a blue streak for at least a quarter of a mile. Although the spark maybe gone from their marriage it's been replaced with a bonfire of resentment."

With his eyes tearing Sheri asks, "Whatever happened to spike?"

Alex then explains, "Littea does tolerate the creature however on those occasions when Spike climbs into bed with them she'll pick up a few misguided quills. Then as expected both man and beast are promptly expelled. As in all such matters they make their way over here knowing they have a standing invention. The following morning Littea will have her quills, excuse me Spike's removed, then things return to normal, promises are made and the two rogues follow her home."

"With that said I've devised a method of determining if she's had an altercation, I call it the Littea Barometer. It goes something like this, if her approach to the Lodge has a girlish bounce you're pretty safe, however a commandant's stride indicates spike has misbehaved one way or another, and she's had enough." Both men realize time hasn't stood still and agree they better get some sleep, for the trip around the lake would take a few hours, and depending on Littea's arrival, their departure is a toss of the coin.

The following morning finds Alex brewing coffee at nine o'clock, far from an early start. Then from the kitchen window he notices Littea making her way across the parking lot displaying a very anxious stride. Seeing the handwriting on the wall he bolts to Sheri's room where he knocks on the door exclaiming, "Sheri wake up, spike hit his mark and she's heading this way, be at the dock in two minutes."

Sheri opens his eyes and realizes its time to panic. Sitting up in bed he familiarizes himself with the surroundings, and recalls the previous night's discussion regarding Spike. Then he shouts out, "That damn porcupine has just ruined my day." Wearing only his jeans he grabs a pair of boots in one hand and a shirt in the other and runs for the dock.

Within a few short minutes Alex is holding the boat steady as Sheri climbs in, then he says, "We've made it." As the boat shoves away from the dock both men seem quite content that they're safe and far from Littea's reach.

They're a few hundred yards from the dock when Sheri asks, "Where does a guy get breakfast out here?" Hunter motions to a cove along the shoreline, saying, "Over there, we'll be able to dock and eat breakfast at Bucks." Alex then explains that after the interstate system was completed fewer trucks stopped at the restaurant so the establishment placed its attention on a family clientele, and had been more successful with dock accommodations, allowing for would-be water traffic.

Once inside the building Buck Thorton the proprietor greets Alex saying, "There must be quite a storm brewing over at Birch for you boys to brave the elements this early."

Alex is accustomed to Thorton's intuitive nature and concedes with a passive reply, "Yah, something's got Littea's goat."

Buck then reveals her plight saying, "John came over by boat yesterday, and was saying the tension inside the house was heating up. So he and Spike took to the waters and headed over hear. You know that stupid animal thinks he's a dog, he was right up there in the bow of the boat with his nose to the wind. Better yet he expects me to serve him, well considering the alternative I haven't much of a choice. Anyway, John was telling me his brother Herb was sick and is staying with them, thereby putting an even greater strain on the marriage. That's the reason Litteas' all charged up. Ok boys, enough said, what's your pleasure?"

After a satisfying breakfast reminiscent of a lumberman's fare both men leave the dining room and proceed through Truckers Row, a hallway where framed photographs of men and semis hang. Sheri's eye catches a picture of his father, Dutch. This experience leaves him with a feeling of contentment, however this isn't to last very long.

As they cut through the surface water on their return trip Alex carefully explains the function of the Adirondack Guide Boat and its characteristic of riding low to the water line. While at the same time having the capability of carrying two men and their prey, usually a deer. Sheri then interrupts Alex's presentation, saying, "I have to apologize those photographs brought back a flood of memories, especially when Dutch would make round trips, carrying two logbooks to earn enough money for my medical school tuition. It must have been quite a disappointment when I decided to enter the seminary."

Sheri says very little for the next hour leaving Alex wondering how long he can keep up a one- sided conversation. Then with the outing coming to an end Hunter voices his concern, saying, "You'd make a lousy major league umpire, he's safe, no wait a minute I think he's out. Stop the bullshit, you're taking a helluva beating for no reason, back then you made the call as you saw it, it's that simple. Your profession speaks of the Spirit of Creation residing in the present. That being the case He was with you as you made that decision, and if He's with you now what business do you have living in the past. That's why you were feeling uncomfortable, you're living there all alone, for He's always in the present! Those days were gone with the setting sun. Anyway spiritual intervention doesn't take place somewhere in the sky, it happens right here in our hearts, that's where the Spirit of Creation works its magic. As each life touches the other a little bit of that Divine spark crosses over, as long as you let it. Then after that transformation has taken place each of us is capable of contributing their share to the betterment of humanity. Stop feeling sorry for yourself and start walking in the presence of today's light."

Sheri sits there lost for words, then after a minute of reflection he's finally able to say, "You're absolutely right, I'm so busy dealing with other people and telling them how to run their lives I forget mine needs attention too. You know, just a week or so ago I decided to look at my career and where it was going, then this assignment came up and I lost interest, maybe I'm on track again. I see now there's a need to take the knowledge and understanding of my medical training to others. I've been living in such a ritual maze, going through the motions without caring to understand the diversity there is in society and the impact it's having. Thanks for the lecture." With a sense of gratitude Sheri takes the oars and rows toward the shoreline.

Sheri has carried this profound feeling of guilt for years, thinking his medical training was wasted. Now he realizes the only way to make amends is to take that knowledge and apply it to some useful purpose. The only question is would it take a career change.

That evening Sheri joins Alex in the game room and sits down at a nearby table, saying, "Would you like some company?"

Alex smiles and then replies, "Sure, I've been meaning to tell you we're indeed having company this evening, the Milner's are stopping over to play cards. John's having a problem dealing with Herb and his medical condition, so Littea asked if they could come over hoping that might help."

Sheri encourages the idea saying, " I can see how that would help, hold it right there." Alex takes on the appearance of a cherub as he sits there displaying an innocent look. Then Sheri exclaims, "What you're really saying is I'm going to meet Spike!"

Alex continues to smile as he replies, "There's really nothing to be concern about, if a point needs to be made you'll know who's making it."

Sheri then cries out, "Seriously, I have a real fear of that animal."

Alex sees an opportunity for a little amusement and says, "You have nothing to worry about, with all that medical training to fall back on you certainly could handle a little thing like a Quill removal."

Sheri plays along with Alex's performance saying, "I was there right along with foot extraction." With both men now laughing they enter the game room with their refreshments and begin preparing for that evening's card game. Then as they were about to finish a knock comes from the front door. Alex walks into the adjacent room and welcomes their quest while Sheri takes a seat at a nearby table. Voices are now heard echoing from the Great Room, Sheri patiently awaits a formal introduction that would include his sole source of anxiety, Spike. All enter and exchange hospitable greetings with the exception of their rogue companion who scurries to a well-placed blanket near the fireplace. Sighing in relief Sheri remarks, "He's well behaved." At which point everyone seats themselves at the table dismissing the comment due to spike's poor track record.

After playing a few hands John leaves the table feeling uncomfortable, pouring a cup of coffee he reclines in a nearby chair saying, "This issue with Herb is starting to bother me, he's never been sick a day in his life. You'd think being a logger would had given him an edge, I don't understand any of it!" Just as John was about to finish the telephone rings. Alex answers the call and quietly informs Sheri that Brian Farmsworth is on the phone and wishes to speak with him. Sheri then excuses himself and takes the call in the privacy of the den.

Sensing something was wrong Sheri lifts the receiver from its base and asks, "Brian, is everything alright?"

In a frightened tone Farmsworth details the events of that evening saying, "I've been informed the staff has transferred Burtrom to a psychiatric ward. It seems those outburst he's been experiencing were bothersome to the other patients." As this turn of events unfolds Sheri instructs Farmsworth to stay with Burt and first thing in the morning he and Alex would leave for the hospital.

Sheri hurries back to the game room where he listens to John as he continues to say, "Herb's barely holding things together. The doctors talk a good talk but when the bills go out the bottom line is their profit margin. I thought their motto was to do no harm! He's worked hard all his life supplying timber so they could build their three hundred thousand dollar homes, and now there's a price tag on him!" Sheri feels his spirit recoil, for that's the very reasons he abandoned the medical profession, profit took priority over the health care of the patients.

After their guest had returned home Sheri vents his frustration, saying, "You know Alex there's some truth to what's been said this evening. Those assembly line physicians are so wrapped up in politics, there really afraid of upsetting the status quo, so they go along with what's happening, and to justify their part they focus on the profit margin because it's a business."

"Then in the case of Burtrom if they can't explain an illness they'll classify it as psychological or chronic without looking into the root cause of the condition. Its all bull shit if you ask me!"

Alex remembers the telephone call, and asks, "Does this have anything to do with Burtrom?"

Sheridan agonizes over an explanation and finally says, "You're damn right, they've got him in a locked ward, and probable heavily sedated, all of which means one thing they're managing the situation and not treating it!"

Hunter seizes the moment by saying, "Hold that thought, O'Daly's empowered you with his authority to find out what's going on, and to make sure the man is comfortable, use your medical training to achieve that goal."

A sense of serenity fills the room as Sheri makes a conscious commitment to care for Burns. Now with renewed confidence he says, "Alex, first thing tomorrow morning call Doctor Middleton and inform him that we're discharging Burtrom and we should be returning here around three o'clock. Also let him know we'll need medications, I'll have Farmsworth fax Burt's medical chart to his office, that'll help with the decisions he'll be making."

Although Alex is impressed with Sheri's assertiveness, he begins to show concern saying, "There could be some political fallout, some of those doctors have a real pompous ego, step on their tails and they'll squeal like pigs."

Sheri smiles then says, "Yah you're right and some need a real ass kicking! I just had a thought, maybe O'Daly was afraid Burtrom was going to be victimized somewhere down the line and wanted a team in place to deal with the situation." As both men agree lightning bugs can be seen flickering their essence on the opposite side of the screen window indicating the evening had extinguished itself thereby allowing each man to bid the other good night.

As the hours pass so does Sheri's ability to sleep, he now begins to feel the weight of Burtrom's problems, then there's O'Daly's faith in his ability to mastermind this project. If anything happens to jeopardize Burtroms recovery it would rest with him in the end. He looks for reassurance, and remembers something Dutch had said, "Do the best you can and take pride in whatever you do. That's all anyone will ever expect."

Chapter Six

Little time is wasted the following morning, with a quick breakfast both men are soon en route to St. Jonathan's Hospital with Alex asking, "What do you suppose is wrong with Burt?"

Sheri adjusts the rear view mirror and then replies, "I've been wrestling with that most of the night, and the best I've been able to put together is some sort of trauma, maybe the aging process or even an overlooked pathogen. It's going to take time, plenty of luck, and Burtrom's help, if we're ever going to find out what's been going on. That includes reviewing all his medical records, we'll have to see if anyone's ever taken a personal history. Sometimes things are missed due to discretion, and we're not going to tolerate that, the man's life depends on what we find."

The Camero now jettisons black carbon exhaust as Sheri turns onto route 87. With the carburetor having now adjusted to the proper throttle setting there's nothing between them and their destination except a smooth ride.

With the two hours of driving out of the way Sheridan finally pulls underneath the hospital's canopy and instructs Alex to wait in the car. He then makes his way to the floor where Burtrom's room is located, and pauses at the doorway listening to Doctor Keno as he instructs the medical students who are accompanying him on hospital rounds, "These are classical signs of alcohol abuse and shouldn't--."

At that moment Sheri bolts into the room, and brushes Keno aside saying, "You're an arrogant son of a bitch."

Keno now shows signs of embarrassment and demands respect saying, "See here Father Sheridan, I'm a physician, and want the respect that goes along with that station!"

With his eyes glowing emerald green Sheri retorts, "When hell freezes over." Keno is clearly incensed and excuses the medical students while Sheri removes Burtrom's i. v. tubing. Later on Sheridan recounts Keno's behavior was that of a spoiled brat, who wasn't getting his way. Meanwhile as these events were unfolding, Farmsworth a would-be spectator is enthralled with the spectacle and awaits a victor to emerge. Suddenly Richard Post walks through the doorway with Keno saying to him, "Restrain this man immediately he' s a threat to my patient!" Post calmly walks over to Sheri and whispers a few instructions. Now with Richards approval Sheri retrieves a wheelchair from the hallway, and with Brian's help removes Burtrom from the room.

Keno is embittered with Richard's actions and reiterates his demand, "I asked you to restrain Sheridan!" With a sense of satisfaction Richard replies, "The threatening party's been restrained, what's your problem?"

While Brian waits at the elevator with Burtrom he repositions the old man's blanket then looks up at Sheri saying, "Did you see Keno's face when we wheeled Burt out of that room?"

With his face flushed from the adrenaline pumping through his system Sheri finally exclaims, "Yah, this was the easy part, now comes the impossible, finding out what's wrong with him."

As Keno and Post walk past the elevator, Keno stops him right there in the middle of the hallway and is heard to say, "I'm holding you personally responsible!"

Richard is fed up with Keno's attitude and makes eye contact with him saying, "Listen I've had enough of you and your whining, step aside or I'll walk over you!" As Post rushes past the trio entering the elevator Keno is seen floundering in his own wake.

Within minutes Burtrom is comfortably seated in the camero, and Sheri's about to open the driver's door when Brian remembers the matter of Burt's medical chart. And yells out, "David I'll fax his chart to Doctor Middleton's office this afternoon and I'll mail the medical records within a day or two." With a nod of acknowledgement Sheri drives away.

On their way back to Route 87 Alex inquires as to the matter in which Burtrom had been released, "What happened in there?" With some hesitation Sheri details the events of his emotional insurgence with Keno, then ends his report saying, "It was over before I knew it, I suspect it was more instinct than anything."

Alex's is worried instinct isn't going to be enough and says, "There could be some crossover in disciplines, remember Father Confessor has been benched, put the white coat on, you've earned it." In Sheri's mind Hunter is right, he has to stop thinking as a priest and concentrate more on medical disciplines, there's too much at stake, Burtrom's welfare for one thing, and another is Richard' s reputation and career. With the probability of Keno demanding an inquiry a certainty the die is now cast leaving Sheri with not only the responsibility of Burtrom's health care but also with putting an end to this enigma. With that said the threesome continue driving Northbound, Sheri focusing on Middleton's visit, Alex on the scenic view, and Burtrom seemingly quite content with just being there.

With the journey almost over there's a hurried stop at Doc Middleton's office, where Sheri is informed by Karl's wife Carol that the Doctor is visiting Herb Milner. She then suggests taking a copy of Burt's chart back to the Lodge, while reassures him Karl would stop by the Lodge immediately after Herb has been examined. Returning to the car Sheri notices Burtrom is exhibiting signs of exhaustion, leaving him anxious to resume a recommended course of medical treatment. So with few options now available he opens up the Camero's four- barrel carburetor for the remaining ten -mile stretch back to Silver Lake.

As Sheri parks the car at the front entrance to the Lodge he looks up in the rear view mirror and notices a refurbished rescue ambulance pulling up alongside the Camero. Alex is eager to renew their friendship and suggests they meet Karl away from Burtrom, as not to make a disturbance. Approaching the ten year old rescue wagon they hear him saying, "It's not going to hurt forever. Anyway it's your own damn fault, all you had to do was stop when spike wanted to, but you continued, what do you expect he was cornered! I've had it, no more of this hide and seek business with that stupid pin cushion, what am I saying, we both know who the stupid one is!"

Alex waits for the conversation to end then hesitates as the passenger door seems to open by itself, then Laddie a black and white Border Collie lunges in the direction of a strip of grass where he begins rubbing what appears to be a wounded face. Karl is frustrated with the dog and joins Alex and Sheri standing just a few feet away saying, "You'd think after one episode he'd learn his lesson. Hello Alex, Doctor Sheridan it's a pleasure to make your acquaintance, Carol telephoned while I was finishing with Herb, saying you would- be heading over to Birch." Looking over at Burtrom he continues, "Shouldn't we get the old boy to his room?"

Sheri doesn't want to frighten Burtrom and replies by saying, "Burt's been through the wringer, we'll need to exercise a little forethought as not to alarm him, who knows how he'll react." Karl agrees then approaches the old man whose now repositioning himself in the rear seat of the Camero.

Burtrom is determined to be recognized, and shouts, "I want to get out of this damn sardine can!"

Karl eagerly holds the car door open while the old man makes his exit. With his legs weakened from the ride Burtrom holds onto the door demanding accountability, "What in the world is going on, and who the hell are you?"

Sheri and Alex now join Karl as Burtrom continues his inquiry while leaning against the car for support, "I want answers, and I want them now!"

Sheri steps forward saying, "You've been at risk for being overmedicated, and if you're to make a beneficial recovery it'll be done under the watchful eye of Doctor Middleton. Needing to reassure Burtrom, Karl explains, "It's understandable that anyone in your position would have intense feelings toward this situation. You've been bounced around with little insight as to what caused your health problems. However I need your cooperation if you're to get well, if not I'll have to return another time when I do have that assurance."

The old man is confused as well as exhausted and concedes the argument whereby allowing Alex to escort him back to the Lodge.

Sheri and Karl now watch silently as both men make their way into the building. Then Sheridan turns to Karl saying, "Well it looks as if the game is being played in on our court now."

Karl realizes the magnitude of the challenge and replies, "I know what you're saying but it's going into overtime and from what I can see people are getting tired." With guarded optimism the two men gather Burtrom's chart and Karl's medical supplies. Then with a sense of urgency they enter the retreat whereupon Alex joins the procession into the den.

For the next hour an intense review of Burt's chart takes place with Middleton and Sheridan discussing Burtroms medical condition, while leaving Alex wondering what direction Burtrom's stay at the Lodge would-be taking.

With the uncertainty of the moment showing on Karl's face he walks across the room and looks out a nearby window saying, "We have a very delicate course of events ahead of us. Some known, others obtuse, and we're going into this exercise without a blessed clue as what needs to be done. If you have any ideas this is the time to speak up!"

Lifting himself from one of the overstuffed chairs Sheri reaches for Burt's chart, saying, "The perfect place to start is right here, we'll implement a medical protocol, stabilize his condition and take it from there."

Karl then replies, "Alright we'll continue antibiotic therapy for another ten days and gradually reduce his antidepressant medication over the next few months to where he feels comfortable. Maybe by then we'll have a handle on what's been going on."

Alex is seated in an adjacent chair fingering a table lamp made of deer antlers and begins to say, "I've been around Burtrom for nearly six months and in that time I've never seen him display interest in anything."

Sheri realizes Alex's insight may have merit and glances in the direction of a bookcase spanning the length of the entire back wall. Walking over to the shelves he makes a selection entitled {T. Green Personal Journal 1950}, then he says, "There's one for each year starting with 1900. Oh my, there's a complete collection of the classics, this is just what the doctor ordered, and with his knack for organization Burtrom would-be more than willing to catalogue this collection. We would then be achieving our primary goal of strengthening his cognitive abilities." With an achievable goal in place Karl gives his approval to the plan and then leaves for home.

That evening as Sheri and Alex begin playing cards the telephone rings, and interrupts their game. Alex answers the call and hands the receiver over to Sheridan who then listens to Brian recalling the events of that afternoon, saying, "Sheri you certainly caused a stir, Keno is madder than hell, and is threatening to hold both of us accountable. He's even made a request that an incident report be filed, saying he'd go high if need be. I don't know what that means, unless he's thinking of going high up the ladder. We're in a fine mess!"

Sheri roars with laughter and then offers a few words of comfort, saying, "Brian your colors are showing relax, take a deep breath and think. If Keno does complain to the Chief of Staff it'll end there, we're operating under the authority of John O'Daly, the man who signs everyone's pay checks."

There's a pause in the conversation followed by a sigh coming from Farmsworth. Although he's now composed Brian still feels uncomfortable, and replies, "I'm not at ease around controversial issues." Sheri knows he's taken most of the heat that day and offers a suggestion, saying, "You've been through the mill, stop thinking and get some sleep. We'll deal with one crisis at a time." The conversation concludes with Brian assuring Sheridan the medical records belonging to Burtrom would- be on their way to the Lodge within a day or two.

Chapter Seven

Two days later the medical records arrived by courier as promised, however their review has to wait, for Sheri and Alex have been tending to Burtrom's personal care, and with Doctor Middleton stopping by daily there's little time left for anything else.

Wednesday morning of the third week everything changes. Burtrom's infected leg begins to show sighs of enough improvement where Sheri and Karl can now make their systematic review of Burtrom's complaints. Then as the exercise is about to finish Karl stands-up and stretches his legs, saying, "Well Sheri, I'll have to agree with Doctor Keno, Burns does show signs of alcohol abuse."

Sensing defeat Sheri leans forward and begins massaging his brow saying, "It looks like I'm ass deep in alligators!"

Karl dismisses himself and begins walking toward the door saying, "I could be wrong, this isn't a perfect science, with that said my money is on Keno's diagnosis. I have to rush, I'll be checking in by phone Friday as to the progress Burtrom is making."

Alex steps aside as Karl leaves room and then he says, "I was about to offer you guys lunch, what's up?"

Sheri returns the medical records to their folder saying, "It appears Keno's right and Burtrom's is experiencing signs of alcohol abuse!"

Alex retorts, "You're shooting from the hip, Burtrom deserves something better than that. Anyway, you've arrived at a subjective conclusions, take some constructive criticism stay away from conjecture, and other peoples opinions. Start thinking for yourself, and stay focused on the facts that you've been drawn to, then come to your own conclusion!"

Sheri seems embarrassed as he replies, "You're right I was allowing Middleton to do the thinking, leaving me wide open to their opinions."

Wanting time to rethink the issue Sheri continues, "How about taking a few days off, Littea can come over and pickup the extra slack."

Alex displays a captivating smile and then explains his idea, "I've intended to start a new hobby, let me tell you about it over lunch." With coffee and sandwiches in hand Alex enthusiastically unfolds his artistic venture saying, "First I'll have to fabricate a case to shelter a tape recorder, microphone, and batteries. Then establish sites where solar panels can be used. After that the easy part comes in, collecting the tapes."

Sheri sees an opportunity for a little amusement and asks, "Do you suspect a family of Beavers maybe looking for a bigger lodge and they have their eyes on Birch?"

Alex hesitates for a moment and then replies, "No, but I've heard from a reliable source that an extremely large flock of Woodpeckers has planned a full scale invasion for sometime next month." Both men begin to laugh.

After things had settle down Sheri inquires further into Alex's project asking, "I know you're well intended, but what's the purpose of this exercise?"

Alex then explains the function of the device saying, "Photographs record events for posterity, and if done correctly it's wonderful, however that art form also captures the silence. What I'm trying to do is create an audio picture to complement those still images."

Sheri seems impressed with the concept however fears it may consume more time than it's worth, and says, "That'll require a great deal of effort, where will we find the time?"

Hunter responds in a reassuring tone saying, "That's the beauty of this unit it's self-contained, and being sound activated all we'll have to do is collect the tapes, then we'll be able to start the editing process."

With the project having Sheri's approval Alex now agrees that Littea should watch Burtrom because Adam White would have too far to travel. So later in the afternoon he telephones and asks if she wouldn't mind keeping an eye on Burtrom. Littea is receptive to the request knowing the routine hasn't been broken in sometime.

After breakfast the following morning Sheri and Burt walk across the hallway and into the den. Burtrom stands in front of this literary treasure in disbelief. The anguished expression he's been displaying has now vanished leaving him in awe.

Burtrom's behavior is now reminiscent of a child at play as he handles the texts, trying to reassure himself of their existence. For nearly two hours Sheri sits watching as Burtrom explores the shelves, then as the morning comes to an end the old man falls asleep while sitting in an adjacent chair, at which point Sheri quietly turns off the reading lamp and leaves the room.

Walking into the kitchen he finds Littea and Alex preparing lunch, anxious to learn more about that mornings exercise Alex asks, "You guys have been in there quite awhile, how did things go?"

Sheri is gratified with the results and proclaims, "He's taken the bait, and I might add is hooked. Burtrom has finally found contentment." With that being said Littea begins serving lunch.

With the meal now over everyone sits around for a few minutes in idle chitchat then its down to business. Both men leave the kitchen for the game room where they begin their adventure by carefully aligning all the components for an inventory. Then, when everything has been accounted for the installation begins, and ends three hours later with the completion of the wiring.

Karl telephones the next morning asking about Burtrom, encouraged with the progress he's cautions against overexertion, and then mentions he'll stop over Monday morning. With their affairs now in order Alex and Sheri proceed with optimism not knowing this innocent endeavor would soon end with the possibility of never being recaptured.

During the next two days their electronic device has been relocated four times, first with an attempt at a nearby airfield that had been used by top military brass during World War II. The proximity and its abundant source of wildlife made it an easy choice. The following two locations were the marsh- lands just South of the Lodge, with the fourth two hundred yards North of the hydroelectric station.

With only a few hours needed to set their equipment up the men utilize the balance of each day by using the fishing tackle Alex had brought along. With this being the final day of their excursion Alex once again retrieves his handcrafted fly rod from its case. And with one hand draws fifteen feet of medium weight line from the reel, and with the other gives full animation to the rod, thereby casting his favorite hand-tied fly in an effortless manner.

With their adventure nearing an end, and with only marginal disappointment Alex and Sheri maneuver into the docking area and tie-up.

Later on in the evening an air of contentment fills the game room as the boys listen intently to the tape recorder releasing it's audible images, quite reminiscent of the calm before a storm. As these sounds leave the magnetic tape they capture the attention of crickets on the other side of the screened window, which in turn emanate a response which now can be heard accompanying that days quarry.

As the hours begin to fade Alex says, "These past few days were really enjoyable, but as they say, all good things must come to an end."

Sheri is weary from the day's activities and replies, "You know with Burtrom busy cataloguing the library we'll have more time on our hands. There's enough material in that one room to keep him occupied for the duration of this assignment, leaving us an opportunity to resolve this riddle once and for all." Now with eyelids half closed Alex comes to terms with his own exhaustion, and politely excuses himself for the night.

Sheri is so exhausted he cradles himself in the chair he's sitting in, and thinks if every one could experience such comfort the world would-be far better off. At this point he falls asleep having recaptured the essence of his boyhood thought to have been extinct for some forty years.

The thin veil of tranquility that's been engulfing the Lodge is soon lifted, for at three-thirty the next morning from nowhere a banshee shrill comes from the vicinity of Burtrom's room. In Sheer fright Sheri is catapulted from his chair, a chill now runs the full length of his spine to the nape of the neck. Trying to discern from what direction the disturbance is coming from he takes a brief moment to compose himself, and then races in the direction of Burtrom's room, where he meets Alex already waiting at the door. With the sounds beginning to subside, anguish is now displayed on each man's face as Sheri motions that they should move down the hallway. With adrenaline racing through his system Sheridan exclaims, "A guy could shit his pants over something like this!"

Alex stares in the direction of Burtrom's room and can barely bring himself to say, "It sounds as if things are beginning to settle down." Then with baited breath they wait a few more minutes, and with nothing indicating a further disturbance both men return to the game room.

Alex walks directly to the liquor cabinet and prepares two drinks, and offers one to Sheri. He then draws a chair closer to a nearby window hoping to capture a breeze coming from its opening, and then says, "This business has me rattled, and if you don't mind I'm going to take the edge off the situation with a few of these!" He then numbs the experience by taking another swallow.

Sheri sits in an adjacent chair watching the whisky in his glass intermingling with the water and his thoughts begin drifting to his manuscript and O'Daly's order. Sheri then recognizes he's absence from the conversation and says, "I'm sorry Alex, I wasn't paying attention, you said something about taking the edge off."

Alex mixes another drink and replies, "Look I'm just as tough as the next guy however this thing has me scared, whatever's going on isn't natural, furthermore we're not equipped to handle a situation like this!"

Sheri gives the matter some thought and then says, "Right now we're dealing with fear, and there's nothing to be gain from that. We'll just have to educate ourselves as to the root cause of Burtrom's problem. Remember knowledge is power, and from that comes enlightenment."

Alex is clearly agitated and retorts, "That's well and good for the long run, but we need solutions now, wake-up and smell the coffee, our problem is staring us in the face now, and we don't even know what it looks like!"

Sheri is tired and sees no need to discuss the matter any further, for he knows neither one of them are objective enough to make sense out of anything at this point. Now with daybreak just around the corner each man returns to his room knowing other things besides their sleep had been disturbed that night.

Chapter Eight

A new day appears with the sun's rays blotting out the chill from the morning air while evaporating the dew from the surrounding landscape.

Littea stands at the front door of the Lodge where she notices Karl's rescue vehicle emerging off Portage Road. She leaves the porch and greets Karl in the parking lot as not to disturb Sheri or Burtrom who are still asleep, and says, "Good morning Karl, where's Laddie?"

The old sawbones has half a grin as he replies, "I just mentioned we were stopping by the Milner's, and that mange mutt turned his tail and was out the door. You know Littea he's lacking in social grace, it probable had something to do with

Spike and his wounded pride." As each is having a good laugh Karl looks around, and says, "Where is everybody?"

Littea is unaware of the previous night or its events and responds by saying, "Alex is in the kitchen drinking coffee doing his best to regain some resemblance of sobriety. Sheri and Burtrom are still asleep. You know Karl there's something eerie going on, I can't put my finger on it, but I know its there."

Karl's stomach exhibits a rumbling sound as he says, "Come on Littea bacon and eggs will put a different complexion on the entire affair." With optimism now shining as bright as the new day the pair make their way into the kitchen where Karl notices Alex leaving by the rear entrance. Hunter is in full stride leaving Karl winded just thinking of a chase, and within minutes Alex is at the water's edge looking back at the Lodge.

Karl decides not to pursue his quarry and pours a cup of coffee and just as he's about to sit down Sheri enters the room saying, "It's best if you leave him alone, he needs time to sort things out."

With Littea now preparing breakfast Sheri sits down at the table with Middleton and recounts the events of that night. Karl finishes his coffee and then says, "Look Sheri, there has to be a natural explanation for what went on, otherwise scientific discipline would- be thrown out the window."

Stillness fills the room as both men seek out an interpretation of the events of that night. Then, with a turn of the door handle that silence is broken as Alex enters the room saying, "I could smell the aroma of Canadian bacon all the way from the dock, is there any left?" Littea offers a nodding smile and assures everyone there's plenty to go around.

With everyone now finishing breakfast Karl puts his coffee cup down, and says, "Well, it seems we're all contented with Littea's culinary delights, now lets come to some agreement on what happened last night."

Littea is bothered by the sheer implications of the conversation and interrupts the moment with an anxious tone in her voice, "All this talk scares me, would you please move your carcasses into the den so I can clean up!"

All three men acknowledge the sensitive nature of their discussion and leave the kitchen for the den where they can meet in a more comfortable environment. Then shortly after their arrival Alex confronts the other men saying, "I owe both of you an apology. My conduct last night and this morning was inappropriate, I was frightened and didn't know how to handle the situation." With that being said and Alex having been absolved of his indiscretions everyone sits down and begins examining those events that lead up to Burtrom's disturbance.

After discussing different scenarios for over an hour Karl looks at his watch and realizes he's pressed for time and grabs his bag off the desk saying, "There's nothing new here. You've seen his medical records there's a pattern of occasional disturbances, repeated once again at St. Jonathans. I've a medical practice that needs attention, take the bull by the horns. Watch Burtrom's vitals, and after he's settled into a daily routine, ask for his opinion. When there's nothing's ventured, nothing can be gained, right. Oh, by the way pay close attention to what's not being said, that'll be your cue, chase it down like a dog running a deer. In any event call me on Friday and remember, patience, he's an old man."

Littea brushes against Karl in the doorway as he's leaving and then she exclaims, "Burtrom is stirring about in his room!"

Sheri is well aware of the responsibility O'Daly has left him with and collapses in the chair behind the desk asking, "Alex, why is it always easier for some to give advice, and harder for others to take it?"

Alex knows the frustration Sheri is feeling and replies, "Good counsel comes from experience, and sometimes pride can be an obstacle in taking it."

Sheri opens the center drawer of the desk and replaces his notepad, saying, "You're right, I'm acquiring humility fast, I have more questions than answers, that must mean something." With that said the pair now make their way upstairs and begin tending to Burtrom's needs.

With Burt sleeping in that morning everyone has to adjust to his schedule requiring Sheri and Alex to make the best of the situation in preparing Burtrom for that days activities, while leaving Littea lingering about waiting for an opportunity to clean his room.

An hour or so later all three men walk onto the patio where an abundance of sunlight forces everyone to shield their eyes, Sheri reaches over the table and raises it's umbrella whereby allowing the old man to sit in comfort. After a few short minutes of conversation Littea arrives and begins serving lunch.

With their appetites now satisfied, Sheri says to Burtrom, "Would you like more coffee?"

Burtrom smiles as he places his cup within reach, and says, "Please, you'll have to excuse my manners, I was so hungry, and with such a meal I feel I've embarrassed myself." Looking across the landscape he continues to say, "This certainly is a beautiful day, it's full of fresh air, it reminds me of my youth when I played baseball, centerfield you know."

Stillness descends upon the trio as Sheri recalls Karl's advice, then carefully quizzes Burns saying, "Burtrom, do you remember anything of last night?"

Burtrom carefully folds the napkin that's been draped over his knee and says, "Why are so many people interested in my personal torment?"

Sheri is unable to temper his emotions, and retorts, "Look Burtrom, snap out of this mind-set, we all have problems, including me. I'm under O'Daly's directive's right now, and he's of the opinion there's more to this situation than just a sick priest!"

Burtrom sits there leaning against the table as if it were carrying his burden, and then asks, "What am I to do?"

Sheri is confident he's established the ground rules and replies, "For the time being I'll expect your full cooperation in whatever we ask of you, and as resources become available you'll then be expect to play more of an active role!"

Littea approaches the table just as their discussion begins to tone down and says, "Look boys if you're done eating I'll have to cleanup, I have a life too." Knowing their presence would only hinder her progress the three men adjourn, leaving Burtrom to the sanctuary of the den, while Alex and Sheri find themselves walking towards the lake.

Within minutes of their arrival Alex is walking along the shoreline searching for a handful of flat stones and then he begins skipping them across the surface of the water. Sheri senses he's being ignored and interrupts Alex as he's about to throw another stone saying, "If this attitude of yours has anything to do with Burtrom I'd like to know, because if it does we need to talk about it!"

Alex moves aside, and throws out a perfect five- skipper, saying, "You're damn right, you didn't have to be such a hard ass, he's an old man. Anyway, you're coming across as a third rate dictator without a country, and personally I don't like it!"

Sheri then justifies his tactics by saying, "Burtrom needs reassurance things will workout, its called tough love. Then if we look at the other side of the coin we need the assurance he'll cooperate, remember we're just at the beginning of this venture." Alex is able to see the bigger picture now and begins walking toward a nearby nesting site used for the recording sessions. Sheri feels he's being ignored and yells out, "Did you hear what I said?"

Alex displays a smile just as he stops short of the bushes and then points to the site saying, "There's our answer."

Sheri sees the situation as being hopeless and says, "All right, you have an answer, that's not telling me anything. You'll have to be more specific if I'm to understand what you're talking about."

Alex then explains, "Our problem is nobody knows what's going on at night, including Burtrom. However if we place our device in his room, then as he starts talking we'll have it on tape. All we'll need now is a little cooperation from Burt." With light shining at the end of the tunnel the boys walk along the shoreline discussing the details.

With everyone seated in the Great Room that evening Sheri proposes the idea to Burtrom, saying, "Alex and I believe we've come up with a feasible means in dealing with the sleep disturbance you've been experiencing." Stillness fills the room as Sheri continues, "Anyway, Alex came up with the idea of placing the recorder in your room, hoping it'll pick up any disturbance while you're asleep."

Burtrom is outraged with the idea, and expresses his disappointment saying, "I'm not some damn guinea pig you two can experiment on. I'm surely entitled to some degree of privacy."

Sheri wasn't expecting a negative response and begins to reason with the old man when the telephone rings. Alex walks over to the staircase and takes the call, then motions to Sheri. Once the receiver had exchanged hands Alex joins Burtrom while John O'Daly on the other end of the line says, "Sheri you've certainly stirred the kettle, news of your confrontation with Keno has reached Rome. There's a number of capable people at St. Jonathan's with years of experience, and unquestioned credentials, maybe you should of consulted one of them before you discharged Burtrom!" While Sheri listens to the conversation he begins to feel uncomfortable and questions his abilities, then draws his attention back to O'Daly who says, "Bridle your enthusiasm, you're walking a thin line. Keno's behind the wings looking for any excuse to readmit Burns to St. Jonathan's. In the meantime watch your backside. I'll be arriving in New York Thursday afternoon you can fill me in any time after that. I really need to go now, give my best to the gang." With a quick goodbye the conversation is terminated.

Sheri remains seated in the alcove beneath the staircase feeling isolated more than ever and begins wondering what John's real motives are then he realizes for the first time O'Daly maybe as much an obstacle as Keno.

This new insight renews Sheri's confidence allowing him to make a call to Farmsworth, saying, "Hello Brian, O'Daly telephoned this evening, and I need a favor--"

Brian interrupts the conversation thinking this was a social call and says, "How's John's stay in Rome?"

Sheri's patience is running thin as he retorts, "Damn it, forget about Rome for a minute. John believes the hospital will intervene on Keno's behalf if I fail to produce results with the protocol I've established for Burtrom. With that said I'll need you to keep an ear to the ground, and if you hear anything telephone me at once!" With a few casual comments the conversation comes to an end. With Brian giving this matter his full attention Sheri is reassured and rejoins the others who have been patiently waiting for his return.

Sheri sits across from the two men and makes eye contact with Burtrom saying, "The Bishop has voiced concern that Doctor Keno and the hospital may take legal measures to readmit Burtrom." Both men look puzzled as Sheri continues,

"We'll have to get down to business, and find out what's behind Burtrom and his problems or he goes back to the hospital."

Burtrom is paralyzed with fear, then in a frightful tone he says, "They can't do that, Doctor Middleton is my physician."

Sheri then replies, "They very well could, if we fail in our attempts."

Burtrom is a little more open-minded about the recorder now and says, "I'll give my consent to the recording idea, only if I'm allowed to review the material beforehand. I think both of you boys will agree I have a personal interest in what's been going on, anyway I have a right to know."

An hour later the power source for the recorder has been converted and the unit is placed on a table adjacent to Burtrom's bed. Alex inserts a new tape saying, "This shouldn't bother you, it'll only activate while you're talking, then disengage automatically when there's silence."

Sheri smiles, and then offers a few words of comfort, saying, "This is the first step you've taken toward your recovery, there's nothing to be afraid of." As a sense of serenity airs throughout the room Alex extinguishes the light then the old man pulls the covers over his shoulders and rolls to one side.

113

Sheri now closes the door not only on Burtrom, but also on the anxiety the old man had been experiencing.

The next night is far from successful for Burtrom only reports a few indistinguishable utterances. All of which may have had a purging effect on him for he now seems quite content. However Sheri isn't feeling tranquil at all, and needs to validate Alex's idea. So he telephones Karl Friday morning asking if this method had any merit. Karl is skeptical of any revelation and cautions against any expectations.

With Alex's idea showing little promise Sheri returns to the den and begins a cursory review of Burt's medical records, and to his amazement finds two pages stuck together. He carefully separating the sheets and begins reading a notation made some three years earlier by Dr. Joseph Wallman. Could this be Wally, his roommate from medical school? He then continues reading the summary, with it saying, "This patient shows classical signs of neurosis. Clinical tests are negative, substance abuse isn't indicated, causation unknown. Father Burns care and treatment would -be best served on a routine basis through John O'Daly's office." Sheri emits an exhaustive sigh and then his body forms to the contour of his chair, thinking if Keno only knew alcohol abuse had already been ruled out. The only challenge facing Sheri now is keeping this ace up his sleeve long enough to put an end to Keno's pompous attitude.

Sensing relief Sheridan decides to celebrate with a walk along the shoreline hoping the brief excursion would release the stress that's been building up over the past month. As Sheri walks along the proverbial path less traveled he losses tract of the time and has to retrace his steps which affords him an opportunity to reconsider Burtrom's condition and what needs to be done about it. While approaching the Lodge he notices Littea standing at the rear entrance to the building. A few minutes later as he enters through the kitchen doorway she's heard to say, "I've been looking all over for you! They've been two telephone calls, one from Karl a little after lunch, and the other from Thomas Waters an hour ago!"

Sheri is startled by her behavior and exclaims, "Littea, calm down before you blow a gasket." He then glances at the wall cock and realizes it's already four p.m., and franticly makes an attempt at calling both men. With his efforts being unsuccessful Sheri leaves messages that they're to return his call.

That evening as he's en route to Burtrom's room for a bed check the telephone rings, rushing down the staircase Sheri takes the call in the alcove. It's Farmsworth seeking information about the events of the next day, saying, "Sheri I was informed by Thomas Waters there's a meeting to be held at the Lodge tomorrow, and I'm to attend. Do you have any idea what this is about?"

Sheri replies, "It seems as if we're both in the dark on this one. I do know something is going on because Waters and Middleton tried to reach me this afternoon. You know as well as I there's only one person capable of causing such a fuss, and that would-be O'Daly!"

Brian shows concern regarding John's predictability and asks, "Do you suppose he'll spring something on us?"

With his faith in O'Daly somewhat compromised Sheri turns to the Wallman report for a little security, and says to Brian, "We'll just have to wait and see what develops, and if he does spring a surprise on us we'll live in the solution and not in the problem. In any event one thing you can count on, O'Daly's feeling some kind of heat otherwise he wouldn't be making the trip up here!"

Farmsworth's understanding of the situation hasn't improved so he now inquires into the journey and the best route he's to take. With the instructions taking only a few minutes Sheri terminates the conversation by asking Brian to locate Burtrom's personnel file.

Chapter Nine

While Sheri leaves his room the following morning he glances out the second floor dormer and notices Richard Post's pickup truck, and John O'Daly's sedan parked outside. He hurries downstairs not wanting to be accused of sleeping on the job, and frantically scans for anyone's presence. Then as he's entering the kitchen he encounters Littea drying her hands in somewhat of a frustrating manner, and she says to him, "If you think for one minute that I'm cooking breakfast for some Johnny-come-lately you're mistaken!"

Sheri feels the temperature drop and skirts around the table in the direction of the coffee maker, grabbing a cup he pours it's dark brew, then looking up he sees the poster child for the worse dressed man of the century. Farmsworth then walks through the doorway feeling quite embarrassed, while at the same time trying to explain his attire, "This is the best I could come up with in my size." He stands there dressed in a university sweatshirt, while wearing a pair of tan slacks, saying, "That's all they had."

Sheri displays a robust smile while trying not to laugh, then asks, "Brian, who are they?"

Farmsworth replies with a boyish manner, saying, "The hospital's lost and found department who do you think. With such short notice, I-."

With the situation becoming more uncomfortable Sheri interrupts the conversation saying, "There's a clothes closet downstairs. In there you'll find an assortment of jeans, I'm sure something will fit, and I'm certain Alex has a pair of boots you can borrow."

As Farmsworth heads in the direction of the laundry room Sheri begins exercising his new found culinary talents, only to be interrupted by Littea, who delivers a few well - chosen words before leaving, "I'll expect advance notice in the future if my services are required on Saturday. And as for tomorrow you boys are on your own." She then storms through the doorway slamming the door as she leaves.

Brian makes his way upstairs inquiring as to Littea's unsettling disposition, saying, "I thought the ceiling was going to fall in, what's wrong with her?"

Sheri makes an attempt at exonerating her behavior saying, "She's under a great deal of personal stress, however that doesn't explain her attitude this morning. More likely than not the increased activity around here is making her feel uncomfortable, and that's not entirely her fault. Things seem to be in a state of flux, making all of us a little edgy."

After breakfast both men linger around the table discussing Brian's new assignment, when suddenly Sheri notices activity on the rear patio. Thomas Waters has just left his chair, and appears to be handing out sheets of paper to Alex, Richard, and O'Daly. Sheri's confidence is now beginning to erode, maybe Brian was right, and O'Daly has thrown a curve. With neither man wanting to intrude on the meeting they decide to wash the breakfast dishes, and then visit the Great Room.

Twenty minutes later both men enter the room with Sheri offering Brian a brief tour, which consist of a few waves of the finger, then he sits down to say, "Their meeting has me baffled. You said it yourself, once you've figured the man out he's apt to throw a curve ball, well he has and we're sitting on the bench."

Brian is just about to reply when he hears a heavier tone of conversation coming from the patio. With the session now breaking up O'Daly and his entourage enter the building, and within minutes John's discerning eye catches Sheridan's silhouette. Then he dismisses the others and says to Sheri, "Sit over here, I want a word with you." Sheri feels as if he's about to be reprimanded and jockeys for a defense, then O'Daly says, "I'm afraid you have the wrong idea, that meeting this morning had nothing to do with you." Sheri leans back and exhausts a sigh that can be heard from across the room. O'Daly roars with laughter as he says, "You have to learn how to relax my boy." Then he continues with an explanation of the morning's events saying, "Over a hundred years ago the elders of this Native-American tribe, and Church leaders had a falling out of sorts. You see the Bishop at that time was less sensitive to their traditions, so without any formal resolution being made I initiated a dialogue of sorts with Alex's grandfather. Of course we have a few hurdles to cross, but I'm certain with a little more preparation we'll be able to work something out. So that's, that. You'll have to excuse me, there's paperwork needing my attention, we can continue our conversation over lunch. By the way I understand the fare will be sandwiches, potato salad and chips. Too bad Littea's off tomorrow, I guess we'll have to learn to enjoy our own cooking." With briefcase in hand O'Daly walks in the direction of the den to finalize the draft he's been working on.

With everyone having finished his delicatessen style lunch O'Daly announces there's to be another meeting and leads the group into the den. O'Daly seats himself behind the desk and instructs Richard to secure the door. Then John commences with a silent roll call, which intimidates his audience. Finally he focuses his cross hairs on Farmsworth who's seen this tactic before, and repositions himself in the chair he's seated in, allowing O'Daly just enough time to play his hand, by asking, "Brian, what's going on with Keno?"

Brian straightens his posture then replies, "He's still adamant about the issue, and has developed a following all of whom want the matter persuade."

O'Daly is clearly agitated, and displays a frown as he continues, "Ok, Richard, if you were me what approach would you take?"

Richard is quite comfortable with the question, and says, "File a counter-complaint stating the reasons why Keno's treatment plan was inappropriate, and how it was placing Burtrom at a greater risk for complications."

O'Daly now pans his line of vision in the direction of Father Burns and hesitates for a brief minute then asks, "Burtrom what's your take on this?"

The old man smiles and then says, "I'd like to see his goose cooked!" At this point everyone in the room breaks out in a roar.

John has to restrain himself from laughing then he calls the meeting to order saying, "Alright, enough is enough, you've had a good laugh."

Burtrom now feels he's among friends, and continues to say, "Yes, that would do nicely, then everyone can have a piece of him."

O'Daly is unable to contain himself and begins laughing, wiping the tears from his eyes John says, "Ok gentlemen, we have business to attend to, you're next Sheri. If you were calling the shots what would you do?"

Sheri isn't ready to discuss the Wallman Report, however he does offer support for Dick's plan saying, "I would first apply Richard's solution to their complaint. Thereby allowing us enough time where we can review Burtom's issues, and maybe by then we'll have a better understanding of the situation and what remedy we should be looking at."

Richard interrupts Sheri's presentation and addresses O'Daly saying, "If you remember we were acting under your explicit authority when this was taking place."

O'Daly replies, "That's beside the point. We still have two medical opinions at the time of this incident, one from a licensed physician, and another from a medical doctor who never went into practice. How would it look if Keno prevails in his argument, and we lose Burtrom along the way, gentlemen we can't let that happen."

With everyone feeling uncomfortable Farmsworth suggests they step outside for a little air thereby fostering a new perspective of the situation.

With drinks from the kitchen the men pair themselves off on the rear patio in idle chitchat. The exception to this is Sheri who now says to Post, "Richard I want you to listen carefully, Burtrom had received a proper diagnosis some three years ago, however it never went any further than that." Leaning over the railing as if to secure more privacy he explains the importance of the Wallman report.

Richard then replies, "O'Daly has displayed confidence in what we're doing, if we keep this from him who knows what will happen!"

Sheri defends his position saying, "It's in our interest if we pick the time for any disclosure especially this one. I intend to present an image of O'Daly that will place Keno on the defensive, thereby allowing us to go on the offensive in proving Wallman's diagnosis was correct, an end run of sorts. Anyway, if John knew what was going on he'd be running the show, and everyone knows what that's like."

Richard knows the nature of O'Daly's temperament and replies, "A bull in a china shop, and that's something we have to avoid at all cost."

With everyone more relaxed they regroup in the den with O'Daly saying, "I've had an opportunity to listen to your ideas, and this is what we're going to do. Thomas, you'll work with Richard on drafting a rebuttal, Brian you'll standby in case you're needed. Sheri, you and Alex continue assisting Burt in his recovery." Then O'Daly gives Burtrom a commanding stare and says, "I insist you give these two men your full cooperation." John pauses long enough to read Burtrum's expression then he address the others saying, "Karl's absence makes our task a little more difficult, with that being said we'll have to find a way where he'll be willing to help."

Sheri responds by saying, "I'd be happy to talk with him, he's a reasonable man, and if I reassure him of our limited expectations he's apt to be more receptive. Then we'll have the best of both worlds, the man, and his connections."

As the meeting comes to an end O'Daly says, "We could have a rough road ahead of us, however if we fill-in a few potholes we may find the ride enjoyable. One more thing, I'm meeting with the tribal council tomorrow, any of you wishing to attend are welcomed." Alex motions to O'Daly in an attempt to get his attention, and he does with John saying, "Oh, I almost forgot, Alex and I are going fishing this evening, and you're all invited, oh, make sure you bring your own bait."

With the sun now settling behind the mountains it's fading glow begins to cast pastel colors over the boat and the men in it. Without expectation the excursion produces more fellowship than fish. There's the occasional cast, along with an infrequent strike, however the most important thing happening is an investiture of sorts involving each man to the environment, which ultimately has a purging effect on everyone's unconscious conflicts, freeing each man to pursue the activities of the next day.

As the complexion of the woodlands changes to a darker hue, Alex suggests they row back to the docking facilities. With everyone now exhausted the walk back to the Lodge seems endless, however once there O'Daly seats himself in the patio area and invites Sheri to join him, while the others call it a night. Then John looks up at the stars and says, "You know kid, after being installed as Bishop I realized a crystal ball didn't come with the job. So I diligently accepted each challenge as they developed, most with success along with a few disappointments, that is until this evening. While I was out there on the lake all that changed, the prestige along with the problems were of no importance, I felt energized enough to go a second round without all that political garbage I was carrying the first time. Anyway, I can't fully explain the experience the only thing that comes close is some kind of spiritual metamorphosis, oh well, maybe in time I'll be able to understand the implication."

Sheri fails to understand the significance of John experience and says, "Maybe you were caught up in the moment."

John pauses long enough to collect his thoughts and then replies, "No, nothing like that. It's more complex, and if I was honest with myself I'd have to say this experience has something to do with Burtom."

Years later O'Daly remarked to a friend that this day was the beginning of a renewed spiritual life, and would help him explain why so many generations had been swept away by unseen forces.

Sheridan dismisses O'Daly's comments as trivial, and politely excuses himself and then walks into the game room to join Brian.

Sheri enters the room and watches as Brian plays a hand of solitaire. He now looks over Brian's shoulder saying, "Black eight on the red nine."

Farmsworth looks up and says, "Thanks, but this happens to be a no-brainer of a game, I didn't need your help!" Brian now gets up and walks to a nearby table and retrieves a folder then hands it over to Sheri saying, "This is Burtrom's personnel file. I'd like to know one thing why didn't you have Tom Waters make this delivery?"

Sheri replies, "If my request had gone through Tom, O'Daly would had learned about it and sensed something was going on. Then a barrage of questions would of followed leaving me in a compromising position where I would-be expected to explain myself, this way I avoid all of that."

While Brian is dealing a new game he asks, "Do you know what you're looking for?"

Sheri clutches the file under his arm, and replies, "I haven't a clue, but I suspect whatever's going on probably has its root somewhere in these pages." Brian expresses his indifference by saying nothing as Sheri leaves the room to review the records.

After breakfast the next morning O'Daly and his entourage drive into the village where they meet with the tribal counsel, introductions are made, followed by casual conversation, thereby setting the tone. Then ceremonial gifts are exchanged with the pronouncements of good will, at which point all tension has vanished, leaving everyone at ease. However, all too soon both groups express sorrow that the gathering was coming to an end, especially with all parties now feeling comfortable with one another.

With the agenda finally being met John, Richard, and Tom Waters return to Albany. Brian on the other hand is uncomfortable with the idea of driving in O'Daly's shadow so he stays behind long enough where he can put distance between himself and the others.

Later in the day Burtrom looks for a little seclusion and begins walking in the direction of the abandoned airstrip near the Lodge. There he finds peace and contentment something he hasn't experienced in years. However he's not alone, Sheri is watching his charge from a second floor window, while at the same time reviewing the events of that day, and wonders if these Native-American's could contribute anything towards Burtrom's recovery.

While all this is going on Alex walks through the front doorway and notices Sheri sitting at the second floor dormer and says, "I've been looking all over for you."

Sheri divides his attention between Burtrom and the conversation saying, "I've developed a few ideas and would like to discuss them with you sometime tonight, however, right now we have to prepare Burtrom lunch."

Burtrom is finally persuaded to leave the serenity of the landscape, but before doings so he says, "You boys should take a few minutes and smell these flowers."

Later that evening Alex leads Sheri into the den, where both men begin tying flies. After an hour of demonstrating his skills Alex collects the few he's made, and suggest using them on their next excursion. He then walks over to a nearby window and raises the bottom sash, allowing a gentle breeze to enter the room. Alex stands there at the window watching a deer running along the shoreline then remembers the discussion they're to have, and says, "You mentioned this afternoon you've developed a few ideas." David says nothing as he makes an unsuccessful attempt at tying another fly. Alex then gazes in the direction of the lake, and is awe-struck by the moon's radiance over the water, then, in a commanding tone he says, "Come on Sheri don't leave me in the dark."

Sheri walks over to the desk and removes Burtrom's personnel file from the left drawer and shows the contents of the envelope to Alex saying, "Within these pages is a medical report completed by Doctor Wallman which exonerates Burtrom from Keno's diagnosis of alcoholism." Sheri then returns the document back to the drawer and both men now head in the direction of the kitchen where Littea's homemade banana bread can be sampled. Sheri offers Alex a slice along with an explanation of the Wallman report. Alex then inquires as to how it was found. Sheri finishes his snack, and then explains the matter, and ends by saying, "There's more that has to be done. First we'll have to see if any dots can be connected between Burtrom's medical records and his personnel file, and if there's a match then we'll take it from there."

Alex is encouraged with the idea and says, "I think you might -be on to something however I'm not one who buys into something at face value. I'm more than willing to accept the Wallman report because that deals with fact, but this business of subjective interpretation has me worried."

Sheri returns the loaf back to the breadbox and says, "Alex, of all people you should know how this is to be handled." Sheri tries to stimulate the proud heritage looming within his friend, and says, "Think of this endeavor as a hunt, we'll be watching for signs throughout this journey, always vigilant and ready to respond, its that simple."

Alex is now able to develop a clear image of Sheri's plan, then responds with a smile saying, "It's not that simple. If we're not paying enough attention to our signs we could end up back tracking, and that would-be a waste of time and energy."

Sheri notices the time and ends their conversation saying, "I need to telephone Karl in the morning and see why he wasn't at the meeting. In the meantime we better get a good nights sleep, with that we'll be able to handle just about anything." With nothing more needing to be said each man retreats to their respective rooms for the night.

Chapter Ten

Sheri awakes the following morning and finds a positive change in his disposition affording him the opportunity to proceed with the days activities in a confident manner. Then after he had finished breakfast, Sheri telephones Middleton's office, saying, "Good morning Karl. I hope I haven't caught you at a bad time, but with you being absence at Saturday's meeting we were wondering if everything was alright."

Karl wasn't prepared for this conversation and replies, "I've been giving a great deal of thought to my practice, and what direction it should take. So when O'Daly's office called Friday morning leaving word he expected my attendance on Saturday, I decided there was no need of burning myself out. I'll continue my outreach duties, and hold office hours, however with regards to sundry issues as case studies, and reaching their conclusions that's out of the question, there's no time for that."

With his fears now validated Sheri is left with one option, seeing if Karl would play a limited role, and says, "All we're asking is that you make yourself available, just be there if we need answers or opinions." Karl, not wanting to be perceived as insensitive agrees.

On Wednesday of this week Sheri had another look at Burtrom's personnel file which encompassed his assignments at St. Paul's Parish situated in Stockland just East of the Hudson River and St. Mary's located in Delphi along the Rivers West bank. So with nothing matching in Burtrom's files Sheri telephones Richard Post for assistance, saying, "Good morning Dick. Do you have any idea where St. Paul's parish files are?"

With the situation being what it was Richard is quick to respond, "Those damn cartons are here in my office getting in the way, and to be honest with you I wish someone would come and get them because I can use the space."

Sheri is uncertain as to their number and asks, "Are there more than the three I had packed away?"

Richard chuckles with amusement as he replies, "No, just the three, matter of fact just yesterday I inventoried everything again, it's a perfect match to what you had cataloged."

Sheri is more specific and proceeds to ask, "Would there happen to be any statistical data or progress reports on the list?"

Richard reviews the list once again then replies, "There's nothing like that here, Tom Waters might know how to locate them. Now, about these files, arrangements can be made for their delivery."

Sheri willingly accepts the invitation for delivery, then ends their conversation, thereby allowing him to place a call into Waters office with him asking, "Hello Tom, David Sheridan. Do you know if statistical or progress reports are available for the time Burtrom was pastor at St. Paul's?"

O'Daly's new adjutant is unfamiliar with the many aspects of his position and retorts, "If there anywhere it'll probably be in storage, and I wouldn't expect miracles. The archives department is packed to the ceiling, it'll take a week or more before anything is found. This better be worth the effort I'm busy and shorthanded, when they're found they'll be sent on to you, ok, look you'll have to excuse me, I have to attend to matters here." Sheri now feels as much out of the water as the fishing trophies hanging above him on the wall.

As Sheri ends his conversation with Waters, Alex walks into the room holding a cassette tape saying, "You look as peaked as that large mouth bass."

Sheri smiles and then displays the right amount of humor by saying, "Maybe so, but I'll recover, now what do we have here?"

Alex pulls a chair alongside of Sheri's and replies, "I'm not quite sure, Burtrom handed it over with a look of indifference." Hunter then inserts the cassette into the recorder that's sitting on the desk. As both men heed to the semi-audible sounds being produced they display an awkward look, expressing their own disappointment. With nothing more being emitted from the magnetic strip only one plausible consensus can be reached, the sounds were that of a spirit in torment. With the tape now silent the recorder comes to an abrupt stop disclosing nothing further of that night.

With his expectations now gone Sheri says, "Burtrom is certainly displaying classical signs of trauma."

Alex is now embarrassed his idea didn't workout and suggests preparing a few sandwiches, and discussing the matter over lunch. As the men are seated on the patio Sheri realizes they've distanced themselves from the taping process and says, "You know neither one of us are happy with the quality of the recordings, we'll have to examine other options. Then on the other hand the pace could very well pickup once the files arrive on Saturday, in any event we'll have another start, and that's something both of us will look forward to. The only fly in the ointment is Water's ability to acquire the statistical data, that could take two weeks."

Alex recalls Karl's earlier suggestion and says, "We could approach Burtrom with regards to his thoughts on this matter, he maybe more receptive this time and surprise both of us."

Sheri defends his position, saying, "No. The timing wasn't right then and it's not now. Karl and I are at opposite ends of the fence on this one. Burtron's isn't in a position to interpret those events in his life, and neither are we until more facts become available, no the timing isn't right!"

Alex feels slighted by Sheri's remarks and replies, "We should at least review his personnel file and develop a few workable scenarios."

Sheri takes a few minutes and explains the drawbacks to the suggestion, saying, "That would- be a random start that neither of us wants, and it would eventually end up in simple conjecture leading us in one direction than another, and that's not in our best interest. No we'll wait at least until Saturday, then we'll take a systematic approach." With both men in agreement, each settles back and finishes his meal.

With lunch now over the topic of discussion turns to the two days the men have available and what they're to do with them. Then Alex says, "We'll have a few days to rest, how about coming along with me on Friday then you'll have an opportunity to meet my grandfather? His cabin is just across the lake, and who knows you may just enjoy the trip, it'll only take a few hours, and I'm sure Littea would pitch in and watch Burt while we're gone."

Sheri knows this means a great deal to Alex, so he agrees to meet with Longshadow.

Thursday afternoon arrives with O'Daly telephoning for an update and Sheridan becoming frustrated with his interference, leaving both the men at odds. Sheri then emphasizes the importance of patience, and reminds him this task falls under the heading of divine providence. O'Daly feels comfortable with Sheri's handling of the situation and makes a promise not to interfere in the future. Year's later Sheri recalls finding satisfaction in putting O'Daly in his rightful place, John knew how to dish it out, however this time he found himself on the receiving end and having to take it. In any event the matter was finally cleared up leaving Sheri with the feeling John could do with a little constructive criticism.

Both Alex and Sheri need to get away from the Lodge even if its only for a few hours, so on Friday morning Littea agrees to watch Burtrom while the men visit Longshadow. However she does stipulate they're to return in four hours. With the boys now freed of their obligation they rush to the shoreline and upright one of the boats and float it alongside the dock. Once inside Alex pushes away from the mooring and begins to row in the direction of his grandfather's cabin.

It's nearly an hour later before they're able to beach their boat. Then as they begin to walk along the shoreline they see Longshadow standing on top of the embankment shielding his eyes from the sunlight dancing off the surface of the water. The old man stands there with his silver hair tied back, wearing a white shirt and blue jeans. With his guest still some distance away he hears Alex say, "Grandfather, I've brought a friend along, his name is David Sheridan."

The ten flagstone steps carved into the hillside gives Alex enough time on the ascent to ponder the enormous effort it took as a child to reach the clearing just ahead. Now, as a man with many years of not visiting his grandfather he's able to recognize the breach his generation had created, and wonders if it will ever be bridged. As Alex reaches the clearing where the cabin is situated, he feels embarrassed, for the last time he visited this site the pine trees that stand sentry at each end of the building were barely eight feet tall, and calculating from his position they've grown another seven feet.

As Alex and Sheri walk toward the old man he's heard to say, "Enter my home and let it be as if it were your mother's womb, a place of protection and nourishment." As he leads the pair through the modest living room, Sheri witnesses simplicity and order at it's best, he glances around, and sees only three pieces of furniture. There's a large pegged back armchair that doubles as a recliner, and alongside of that is a table that stands directly opposite a couch that had the capability of being used as a daybed. All of which had been crafted out of maple, with the chair and couch having the appearance of being upholstered in supple deer hide, leaving any decorator envious.

As the three men leave the living room, they enter a rear area of the building whereupon Sheri is left in awe, again in the middle of nowhere is another library with each text perfectly aligned. Across from the interior wall where the books are shelved is an elongated exterior wall enclosed at each end and framed throughout with half a dozen window's which produce a view of a spacious yard that yields to a wildlife trail. Two sashes had been replaced with screens allowing not only for a breeze to pass through, but also for the fragrance of the nearby pine trees, and the scent of freshly cut grass. The old man now motions to the seating arrangements intended for his guest.

After a few moments of reflection Longshadow reaches for a photograph of Alex, saying, "I remember when this was taken, you were nine or ten years old, filled with a fresh spirit." With sadness he continues, "As time passes, our souls wear the years like a laden garment, could it be you're in search of a way to ease that burden?"

Alex marvels at Longshadow's perception, and then replies, "Yes grandfather, it seems the longer I'm traveling life's journey the more I feel inadequate in dealing with its challenges, seldom am I comfortable with the way things are."

Longshadow embraces Alex with great affection and now displays a brilliant smile signifying relief, and then he says, "The journey of souls may take many seasons, we'll travel light, leaving all your wants behind. As a child you knew little, and your needs were supplied to you, so will it be now, the spirit of creation will provide as he does the seasons, and as they pass so will your burden." While Sheri listens he wonders if this could also apply to Burtrom, the similarities were there, but would the methodology be practical.

With time closing in on their visit Sheri interrupts the conversation mentioning an urgency to return to Burtrom's care. Alex's grandfather knowing of this concern says, "Your task is of great importance and needs your attention, I've known of this for many nights, you see the winds have spoken to me of a tormented spirit living at Birch." Sheri, thinking the old man is experiencing a mystical delusion excuses himself as Alex and his grandfather bid one another farewell.

On the boat ride back to the Lodge Alex confronts Sheri, saying, "Dismissing my grandfather's concerns for Burtrom was totally uncalled for, and rude." Sheri is now annoyed, and tries to defend his position by saying, "I was pacifying the old man, be real the wind doesn't talk, you don't expect me to believe that crap!"

Alex knows Sheri's ego is about to be deflated and wants to remember the moment so he stops rowing and looks at Sheridan, saying, "He was speaking metaphorically. You see when conditions are just right, the stillness of the night is broken as sound is carried through the air by the passing of a gentle wind, what grandfather heard was indeed Burtrom!" Sheri has little to say, obviously it isn't polite to speak with a mouth full of humble pie. Silence prevails throughout the return trip and into supper. With nothing further to be said each man postures himself in one way or the other for a defense and without an arbitrator a diplomatic solution would have to wait until the timing was right.

Sheri realizes the importance of making amends so later on in the evening he joins Alex who's already seated on the patio, and says, "Do you suppose Longshadow is willing to forgive my behavior?"

Alex assures Sheri his grandfather had done just that, and explains, "He knows you're not accustomed to nature, or to its mysteries, you'll just have to develop a little patience, and more will be revealed."

Then as the evening drapes its veil on this hot July day, the temperature begins chilling the evening air, leaving an opportunity for each of the men to place their resentments aside and renew their friendship. The conversation now deals with Longshadow, and his ideology. Then suddenly Alex jumps to his feet in excitement and proclaims, "Sheri, look halfway down the North side of the lake where the inlet leads into the marsh, what do you see?"

Sheri makes an attempt at recognizing Alex's sighting, and says, "All I see are intermittent lights, as if someone is signaling, do you suppose they need help?"

Alex roars with laughter then begins to explain, "What you're seeing is a glow from the marsh gasses."

Sheri now exhibits more curiosity while looking at the spectacle then after a few minutes he sits back down again. Alex now feels somewhat vindicated in his grandfather's defense, saying, "I told you about those unexpected mysteries." Both men revel in the phenomenon and its entertainment that is until the exhaustion of the day drives each man to his room.

Chapter Eleven

The first' light' of the following morning dismisses the darkness, and reveals a visible accounting of those chores that need attention. Soon after his breakfast Sheri walks through the front doorway and notices three large boxes placed in a row along the exterior wall of the porch. Sheri realizes Post had kept his word, and with the cartons being too heavy he slides all three over the threshold and calls for Alex, saying, "I need help!"

Alex walks through the dining room and into the Great Room, saying, "I've known that for sometime." He hesitates, then exclaims, "They've arrived!" With the den offering little space it's decided the game room would-be the most logical spot for their storage, while leaving each carton to be opened in their order of importance, thereby making the situation more manageable.

Sheri then decides the next step is to determine the order of importance each carton would have, and to achieve that goal they'd need a historical picture that only Burtrom could provide. And after he had made an accounting of those times they then could reference the events against the items listed in the inventory. Sheri now want's to streamline the process, and says, "Well Alex it seems as if the timing is right, we'll approach Burtrom and see if he'll be willing to provide us with a historical perspective, and maybe then we'll be able to piece thing together."

Alex displays a glowing smile, and says, "We're finally establishing a foothold, the only problem we could possibly have is Burtrom becoming confused with respect to the communities, and their events. That could lead us down the wrong path, then we'll be the one's confused."

Sheri removes an attached envelope from the first box and gives Hunter an encouraging look then seats himself at the game table, saying, "You're right. However with so many facets to this mosaic we'll have to establish a baseline, and that'll come from Burtrom's summary of the way things were at that time. A composition if you will of each community, then we'll have to factor in any sociological impact that might of taken place at the time. With all that we'll have to learn how Burtrom reacted to those events, then we'll see how things match up. That's what I meant by a systematic approach."

Alex is optimistic as to the outcome of this exercise and willing accepts Sheri's strategy, then patiently awaits its implementation.

With a number of hurdles still before them Sheri feels an obligation to forewarn Burtrom as to his role, and says to Alex, "I think Burt would feel more comfortable knowing what's expected of him. I know I would, and who knows he maybe more receptive this time. As for starting, that could take place as early as Monday afternoon, by then he should had adjusted to the idea."

Later that afternoon both men approach Burtrom with their plan, and after giving the concept some thought he accepts the challenge, saying, "These arrangements are far more acceptable than that ridiculous recording idea you fellows concocted." Sheri then cautions the old man it was only one equation of many, and he's to prepare himself thoroughly for Monday's inquiry.

With less than forty-eight hours to prepare for the interrogatories Sheri reviews as much material as time will allow, however with the volumes of files before them the task seems futile. Things aren't moving along even with Alex's help, for neither man knows what he's looking for. Then in frustration they familiarize themselves with only a portion of the files, leaving the rest for another occasion.

With expectations not being met and everyone feeling inadequately prepared they make Monday's objective and file into the den where each man finds his appropriate seat, with Sheri at the desk, Burtrom directly across from him and Alex sitting in an adjacent chair.

Sheri is prepared to take notes and begins by saying, "Burtrom, the reason we're taking this approach is simple, we have all these resources and no way of knowing how they're connected. Hopefully you'll provide an oral history, thereby allowing us to connect enough dots where we can develop a picture."

As in similar situation there's always a potential for an individual to sidestep the tougher issues, and wanting to avoid that problem Sheri confronts the matter head-on, by saying, "There's an enormous amount of time and effort being allocated to this endeavor. So please don't let us down, and remember we're holding the score card, not you!"

A foreboding sensation envelope's the room as each man comes to a personal understanding they've reached a point of no return. Alex gazes through the window seeking an escape from his responsibilities while Burtrom is left alone with his memories. Sheri now waits patiently for Burtrom to collects his thoughts. Then in a quivering voice, Burt asks, "Where am I to begin?"

With everyone feeling somewhat uncomfortable Sheri instructs the old man to start with his appointment as deacon, then he's to include the duties he performed at each parish. Burtrom then proceeds by saying, "At that point in my ministry I was obviously young and in good health, and with everyday being what it was I had everything to look forward to most of all my ordination the following year. That alone should had been of some assistance in the performance of my duties." Burns pauses long enough to drink a glass of water, then continues, "You could say, I was all dressed up with nowhere to go. You see these two pastors, Father Pullman in Stockland, and O'Malley in Delphi were quite accustomed to their roles, and with that being said, each came across as being overbearing. I realize now they didn't have any serious time to delegate my responsibilities, so my assignments fell under the heading of social networking, you know, intervening between the parishioners, and their pastors. Each man in his own unique way seemed to be putting out fires most of the time, and for a while I felt quite inadequate, and wondered if I'd ever make the ranks."

Sheri becomes curious as to the type of problems these two pastors were experiencing, and asks, "Without violating anyone's trust, could you tell me exactly what kinds of issues these men were facing?"

Burtrom collects his thoughts and says, "On the surface there seemed to be an unusual number of counseling sessions during that period. I particularly remember there being many occasion where Father Pullman had to bail several people out of trouble on more than one Sunday morning. These two towns were on an endless roller coaster ride, more so in Stockland, whereas Delphi had it's own set of cultivated problems, which I attribute to it's affluent life style."

Sheri is frustrated with only a partial picture and decides to restate the purpose of the exercise, saying, "Burt, remember that mental image I discussed earlier, it's incomplete, you'll have to step back and describe each town as they were in 1955."

Burtrom begins to show signs of stress however he closes his eyes and begins recalling the post world war II economy, describing each community for better or worse. Then sits there in bewilderment wondering if his ineffectiveness in dealing with these people had contributed to the situation that's plaguing him today.

Sheri fears the old man had taken the wrong path while going down memory lane and says, "Burtrom, are you alright?"

Burtrom's concentration is so intense he's startled into consciousness, saying, "I'm sorry, for a minute there it felt as if it were just yesterday."

Sheri sees an opportunity to learn more, and asks, "What was going through your mind a few minutes ago?"

Burtrom gathers his thoughts once again, then replies, "I was recalling the obstacles I encountered while I attempted to balance the diversity within these communities. Then to complicate matters the diocese eventually combined both parishes. In itself the commute between each town wasn't bad, matter of fact it was a quick ten minutes if you used the Barge Street Bridge. However the social gap could had been measured in light years. It was a continuous battle with Stockland just barely escaping poverty, while Delphi flaunted its wares in front of everyone. If I had to wrap the situation up in one word it would-be dysfunctional."

Sheri sits there in astonishment trying to grasp the complex social conflicts that took place and wonders if these events contributed to Burtrom's condition.

With Burtrom now exhibiting signs of exhaustion Alex feels it's time for a break, and says, "It would-be in everyone's interest if we breakaway from this session, we'll need to examine the facts so we can make an informed decision."

Sheri leans back in his chair, and says to Burtrom, "You sure had your hands full back then, but we're dealing with today and you heard the man its time to wrap things up."

With Burtrom being excused he leaves the den and returns to his room.

Sheri walks over to the opposite end of the room, and stares at a New York State map hanging from the wall. Then he asks Alex, "How long of a drive is it to Stockland?"

Alex looks over Sheri's shoulder and replies, "You know this map is outdated by fifty years, I'm getting the impression we're talking about a two and half hour trip. If we're going we better discuss the matter, meanwhile this room is beginning to wear on me."

With the room filled with memories both men walk onto the rear patio in an attempt to air their discontent. Each man sits in silence, with Sheri planning the trip to Stockland, and Alex struggling with resentments toward those individuals who now occupy his ancestral homeland.

As evening draws nearer each man decides to prepare his own meal, hoping a little space would have a purging effect, whereby allowing them to meet later in the game room. Then at that appointed time each of the men feels a need to address his own personal grievance with Alex being the first to say, "I want this damn thing over with, I have my own affairs to deal with!"

Sheri then exhibits a side of his nature not seen before saying, "Do you consider yourself the center of the universe? Don't you think I'm tired of this crap, babysitting isn't my forte!" Sheri realizes he's out of line, and apologizes, by saying, "Let's take ten, have a drink, and see how this trip to Stockland can be arranged."

Alex wants to put closure to their argument and says, "Look, I need space, that's why I'm living in the middle of nowhere, furthermore I don't feel comfortable dealing with different cultures. Yours had developed from the status quo, and mine with very few exceptions, has remained the same for centuries." Alex has harbored these sentiments for sometime and begins to feel the emotional burden being lifted as he continues, "I'm not going to be entrapped, only to find myself conforming to your cultural ideologies, I'm not your damn sidekick!" Mustering more courage he resumes, "Awhile ago you suggested I think of this venture as a hunt, well to some degree you're right, and if I'm to accomplish that task there's a need to rely on cultivated instinct handed down from one generation to another. Then there comes a time when I have to apply that talent to a specific situation, and I've done that in this case and have come to my own conclusion. I personally don't buy into the Wallman report, or that Burtrom's problems are related to being a priest. From what I can see the diagnosis was politically bias. There's a time and place for reason, but before that process starts open your heart and let the creator speak while your Spirit is still, you'll hear his thoughts! Also, remember this, you're on my turf now, I expect you to respect my heritage, and what I believe, the same way I honor your traditions."

Alex prepares two drinks leaving Sheri confused as to the reason behind his chastisement, then after a moment or two the dust begins to settle, and he says, "I'm sorry I never knew you felt that way."

153

With everything now in the open Alex replies, "I think we both have something to offer, each with his own specific expertise, all we have to do is be tolerant of one another, and work together."

With drinks in their hands both men walk outside where once again the patio offers another spectacular view of the setting sun. Then remembering their unfinished discussion regarding the trip to Stockland, Alex says, "If we intend to visit Burtrom's old parish it needs to be done soon, his condition is stable, requiring little supervision, I'm sure Littea will keep an eye on him, she's scheduled for tomorrow anyway."

With a road trip enabling the men to put distance between themselves and the Lodge Sheri suggests they make preparations, saying, "If we're to leave tomorrow morning we'll need to know what to expect, you better track Burtrom down, hopefully he'll have a little more insight."

Alex displays a renewed interest as he leaves the patio area, and within a few short minutes he's located Burtrom, who seems more than willing to join the group. Once outside Burt places his chair alongside of Sheri's, and sits there seemingly content, and well rejuvenated. While the old man gazes across the landscape he finally says, "I want to thank you fellows for the invitation, isn't this a spectacular view."

Sheri welcomes Burtrom in a matter of fact way instructing him of their intent, saying, "Of course we enjoy your company. But apart from that we're traveling to Stockland in the morning and need a mental image of those characteristics which will help us identify the community."

Burtrom is surprised that Sheri would even ask the question and replies, "You've been there, don't you remember anything of what you saw?"

Sheri responds to the query, saying, "Look Burt, Brian and I were doing what we were told to do, and the only thing of any interest to us was leaving as soon as we were done."

Burtrom has a better understanding of the situation now and agrees to help, saying, "Let's see if I can put this together, you'll travel South on state highway ninety, then drive over to nine-j, at that point you'll see a designated three- mile marker. Then as you drive on you'll see a sign with the Pyxis International Oil and Gas Companie's logo being displayed, the office and tank farm are located off to the right of that. As you continue on you'll find the church to your left, and across the street from that you'll see the town common fully equipped with a statue of a revolutionary war soldier and a cannon. Both the church and common are residentially zoned. Then if I remember correctly there's a little industrial park, situated between Stockland and the Barge Street Bridge which leads you directly into the town of Delphi."

Sheri is intrigued by the complex and asks, "What kind of industries were located there?"

Burtrom struggles for an adequate description of the site, then finally says, "I believe most of those companies were distribution depots that dealt with warehousing and shipping. One company sold composite flooring, and another steel roofing material. Oh yes, I almost forgot, down the road from all this was a ceramic tile outlet. It was an ideal location because the railroad had offered service to all three facilities."

With the landscape now being veiled in darkness and their sole source of information drying up Sheri decides to end the gathering. As the men enter the Lodge they go in different directions, Burtrom to the seclusion of his room, leaving Sheri and Alex to discuss their morning departure in the kitchen. Sheri pours a glass of water and then says, "I hope Burtrom has his act together. If not this trip could be a waste of time, and another disappointment."

Alex smiles and then says, "The worst that can happen is we'll lose's faith in our imagery." Sheri rolls his eyes at which point Alex preempts a possible retort, saying, "I know, think positive, that being the case what time do we leave in the morning?" Sheri allows for some degree of discretion with regards to Alex's ability to convince Littea of their need to make the trip. With the discussion now ended each man calls it a night.

The next morning has an air reassurance to it, giving hope to everyone's expectations. The scene is one of camaraderie, with Littea washing the breakfast dishes, Alex reminiscing over spikes past antics, and Burtrom just listening to the stories and having a good old time.

Sheri has already eaten his breakfast and is now preparing the camero for the trip, minutes later he hears laughter coming from the kitchen and enters the building saying, "Alex, let's get moving, it's already nine-thirty!"

Within minutes of leaving the parking lot Sheri's redlining the tachometer as he shifts into third gear, and as they drive down Portage Road nothing can be seen of the car only an array of sunlit dust particles now trailing behind them. Then the next thirty-five minutes yields little in the form of a conversation, because both men are going through a very private separation process, relieving themselves of Burtrom, and his hardships.

Sheri is preoccupied with his thoughts and finds himself coming out of a road trance, and notices the first indication of interstate eighty-seven just one mile ahead. Now with clear sailing they'll make Albany in an hour and thirty minutes, giving each man an ample opportunity to express those concerns not yet addressed.

Once on the interstate Alex repositions his seat, then asks, "After we've reached Stockland have you any idea what we'll be looking for?"

Sheri pulls into the left lane and passes a tanker on the approaching hill, then, after a few minutes of intense driving he's able to return to his lane.

Alex inquires as to the effort it took to pass the tractor-trailer, and asks, "What do you suppose that truck has for a power plant?"

Sheri displays a reassuring smile, and replies, "His trailer is probably empty, otherwise you would had seen intermediate bursts of exhaust coming from the truck's exhaust stack as the driver shifted gears into the climb." Sheri apologizes for his inattentiveness, and says, "I'm sorry, you asked about something else."

With his attention still on the truck, Alex asks, "What do you expect to find in Stockland?"

Sheri replies, "I'm not quite sure, for now I'll settle for a walk-through, you know, talk with a few people, then size up the situation." Alex is now satisfied there's a game plan in place, and now falls asleep while leaning against his door.

With the number of commercial vehicles now increasing on the roadway Sheri begins maneuvering in and out of the Albany traffic pattern, and begins to encounter the same kind of stress he once did as a professional a driver. He was quite familiar with the road conditions, and the vibration coming from the diesel motors, and transmissions, all of which had a quivering effect throughout his body. Then there was the rough ride coming from the leaf springs, which at times had the capability of lifting him right out of the seat. All this suffering came from hauling freight, and he couldn't imagine the task of driving robust equipment that pulled heavier loads. Although his job was busy, and at times dangerous, it couldn't come close to the demands placed on the transport drivers, for they were a breed unto themselves, taking all the risk hauling loads other companies couldn't, or wouldn't consider hauling.

Sheri remembers making a delivery to such a terminal, and seeing equipment parked in the yard to haul bulldozers, tankers to transport gasoline, flatbed trailers to haul lumber, steel, or anything else left to the imagination.

The hectic pace was one of discipline, for each man knew their equipment inside and out, thereby allowing them to make roadside repairs, freeing them up for another run. All of which left Sheri feeling quite inadequate, however he did respect their independence and ability to make decisions apart from others.

After Sheri had left the Albany interchange he takes the next exit which in time would lead them into Renssalaer, and then onto route nine –J. At this point Alex wakes up exclaiming, "Are we there yet?"

Sheridan now shifts the Camero into third gear, and replies, "No, we still have another forty minutes, you might as well sit back and enjoy the ride."

Alex straightens up in his seat and begins to show signs of anticipation, saying, "You know, this is exciting we'll finally meet people who knew Burtrom, it'll be a homecoming of sorts."

With the sunlight becoming brighter Sheri's attention is diverted away from Alex as he adjusts the car's visor, then he says, "Alex would you do me a favor, and grab the knapsack off the rear seat, and look inside for my camera and any film that might be there. I'd like to take a few pictures of this homecoming, and those individuals who knew Burtrom, anyway the old boy would enjoy looking at the photos."

As the men continue their drive they notice signs of neglect along the highway, with special attention being placed on the three-mile marker leaning to one side. Then within minutes Alex is pointing to a set of gates in front of the Pyxis International Oil & Gas Company. Turning right onto the concrete driveway Sheri stops the car and both men walk over to the secured barrier in disbelief, with Sheri finally saying, "I can't believe this!"

A few hundred feet away are two dilapidated brick buildings, with shattered glass displayed in their windows, now looking across the yard they see grass growing through cracks in the pavement. At the end of the property line is an abandoned railroad siding where rail cars once off-loaded fuel and oil, now weathered rails and empty oil drums rust from years of exposure attest to their abandonment.

Sheri's attention is now drawn in the opposite direction to a landscape dotted with craters, all reminiscent of a battlefield, however there purpose had been to act as dikes containing any spillage coming from the storage tanks. Then in bewilderment he exclaims, "This place has seen better days!"

Alex expresses his disappointment by walking away saying, "There's nothing left here that's worth saving, let's drive into town and find a place to eat lunch."

As the Camero leaves the concrete apron its tires kick up several loose stones, throwing them at a corporate sign attached to the gate. Sheri watches the tachometer as he shifts the transmission into third gear then eyes the odometer, anticipating its reading. Then as the instrument registers its mark he stops the car adjacent to the center- line of the road. Both men sit there looking through the windshield seemingly isolated in time and space, for neither man had been prepared for anything like this.

Then as the shock wears off Sheri drives over to the roadside where he and Alex get out and begin walking across the highway. They now look in a Southerly direction and see a chain link fence bordering the East and West sides of route nine, effectively closing off the boundary to what had been Stockland.

Sheri is disappointed in what he sees and walks over to where St. Paul's Church once stood and sits down on the curbside. Alex catches up to his friend, and says, "Well fella this sure kicks the hell out of imagery." Sheri displays a weak smile, and replies, "I've never seen anything like this, everything has been razed to the ground, there has to be some kind of explanation!" Alex walks back to the car and returns with Sheri's camera, saying, "Here you go one camera, and three rolls of film, let's get busy!"

For the next two and a half- hours Sheri documents their visit with the help of his camera, filming each particular locations he believes to be important, always retaining whatever essence there is within the viewfinder of his camera. Alex is worried he'll run out of file, and voices his concern, saying, "Hold on, you better save that last roll for Delphi."

Sheri realizes Alex was right and returns the camera to its case, thereby ending the discussion. Then in silence both men walk back to the car and resume their trip, with their attentions now focused on Delphi. Then out of no where Sheri makes a U-turn directly in front of the Barge Street Bridge, and rapidly shifts through all four gears. Alex is aging by the minute, and exclaims, "What in Sam Hill is going on?"

Sheri inserts a disk in the CD player, and begins listening to a classical rendition, thereby allowing enough time to pass where he's able to consider Alex's question. Then he says, "I haven't a clue as to what's going on, except to say the entire situation seems strange, leaving me with a feeling we've been suckered into something neither one of us wants."

With his enthusiasm just about gone, Alex expresses his concern by asking, "The last thing we need is another puzzle, assuming you're right, and I'm not saying you are, then where does that leave us?"

Sheri begins to show more tolerance for the situation as he explains, "I think it may have something to do with an experience O'Daly had that night when all of us were on the lake fishing. After we had returned to shore he mentioned something about having some kind of spiritual renewal that involved the environment. I have no idea what he meant by that except to say it primed his consciousness!" Alex wants to understand the significance of what Sheri has to say, and listens as he continues, "Remember that incident where Farmsworth and I were instructed to help Burtrom with the packing up of files, and other parish property that belonged to St. Paul's? Well, in retrospect the oddity seems to lie in Brian and myself being kept out of the loop. We were told renovations would-be starting, and a place was needed to store the material.

Now, after seeing what's left of Stockland I'm very suspicious as to what really happened to the town, and it's residents!"

After the two men discuss the implications of what Sheri had just said they use the remaining roll of film to photograph the Pyxis's Oil Complex, taking pictures of individual compositions that would best illustrate the abandonment. Then after an hour had past the pair can be seen emerging from the rail siding, exhausted, and ready for the trip home.

As Sheri nears the outskirts of Rensselaer he remembers seeing a photo-lab situated in the Shop-Rite Mall that advertised one -hour film developing. He now parks the car at the storefront while Alex takes the film inside for processing, then both men sit down to a belated lunch at a nearby delicatessen.

During the course of their meal Sheri feels a responsibility to inform Alex of an inevitable confrontation that'll take place between himself and O'Daly, and says, "The photographs should be ready by the time we finish lunch. Then we'll visit John O'Daly, and see what he thinks of our photographic skills."

With their meal now over both men stand at the cash register with Sheri paying the bill, and Alex sayings, "Let's see if I've got this right, you're going on the offensive to see what O'Daly knows."

With nothing more needing to be said Sheri holds the door open as they leave the restaurant. Suddenly Alex begins to grin, and then says, "I didn't think you had the balls, but you're setting the old man up, this I'll have to see!"

Sheri now waits in the Camero while Alex proceeds to the photo-lab where he pays for the film processing. After Alex has returned to the car they drive away with Sheri saying, "We'll first confront O'Daly with the pictures, then sit there in silence for as long as it takes. He'll be getting a dose of his own medicine, of course we'll have to be careful, otherwise we'll be the one's with the bitter pill to swallow."

The trip from Rensselaer to O'Daly's office is uneventful leaving both men somewhat refreshed and filled with self-confidence. Then as Sheri drives onto St. Peters Street he notices O'Daly's office window open, and with the temperature in the high eighty's the air-conditioner surely had broken down, Sheri thinks. Both men proceed in the direction of the walkway, where they now walk on the grass, allowing for an element of surprise, for O'Daly's window is directly above the entryway.

As they enter the building little sound is heard as each man creeps down the hallway and into the elevator. Now on the administrative floor extra care is taken not to disturb the tranquility that airs throughout the corridor. They now see Thomas Waters sitting at his desk in the outer office, very reminiscent of a military guard on duty. Sheri now raises his index finger to his lips signaling this sentry to silence. They now make their way into John's inner sanctum and find him seated behind a desk with his collar removed, and sweating profusely. O'Daly holds a handkerchief to his face, as he exclaims, "I concede, I've been ambushed by the notorious David Sheridan!" John emanates a weak smile, leaving Sheri with a portrait of the true man.

With a need to proceed, Sheridan says, "Before we go any further I want to know why you commissioned me to this project!"

O'Daly glances at the wall clock with a compromising expression, and exclaims, "Look at that, it's nearly quarter to seven, we can discuss the matter over dinner."

Sheri, having been a party to this maneuver before, holds his ground, saying, "No, not today John. You've given me an assignment and I intend to carry out your directives, so you might as well tell me what you know!" O'Daly gazes through a nearby window collecting his thoughts while Sheri patiently waits for a reply.

With O'Daly not cooperating, and Sheri's presence now regarded as an inconvenience, Sheridan walks over to where O'Daly is seated. Then says, "Alex and I had the misfortune of having a late lunch, that's why we declined your invitation. You see our preference had been Stockland, however with the lack of accommodations we settled for a restaurant in Rensselaer. The entire situation was bothersome, and we both know what that's like, don't we John?"

As the room fills with silence Sheri realizes there's a need to notify Littea, and instructs Alex to use Water's telephone to make a call, thereby letting her know they're behind schedule. Now, with O'Daly in his proverbial corner Sheridan patiently waits. Then with a blushed complexion John leaves his desk and closes the door, effectively leaving Alex stranded in the outer office with Waters, and O'Daly with Sheridan.

With John and David now isolated in the inner office they engage one another in a stare down of sorts waiting for the other to modify his position. With neither man willing to do so, Sheri hands the photographs over to O'Daly, and with nothing more being said, each man sits down.

O'Daly examines the photographs and breaks down with a sigh saying, "I guess the old adage is true a picture is worth a thousand words." Then he returns the prints back to Sheridan asking, "Where do we go from here?"

With his patience now exhausted, Sheri exclaims, "John, I'm tired of the bullshit, there's no excuse for saying something stupid like where are we going from here. Damn it, where the hell were you when all this was going on!"

The topic of discussion now focuses on Stockland, with O'Daly saying, "I was hoping this matter would- be restricted to Burtrom however it hasn't, so you might as well know." John walks over to a file cabinet and then removes a manila folder from the top drawer, and takes out a single sheet of paper. Returning to his desk he hands it over to Sheri. David recognizes the document as a bill for the demolition of St. Paul's Church, and it's other buildings. Sheri then claims his right to know, saying, "What's this all about? I was under the impression there was a renovation going on."

O'Daly retrieves a box of crackers from his desk drawer and begins to detail each event, saying, "The pledge drive was more than successful. We reached our goal with a little left over, and from all appearances we were ready to start the project. Then a month or so later Burtrom began experiencing one delay, after another. I'm sure his procrastination had something to do with it. That's why I removed him from his duties, I knew something was wrong and I didn't want the man suffering any longer. Then the funds dried up and the rest is history."

As the Wallman report resurface in Sheri's mind he now looks at the situation with a renewed interest, saying, "It sounds as if Burtrom was going through some rough times. Say, didn't the parishioner's have an obligation to fulfill their agreements?"

O'Daly brushes a few crumbs from his shirt, and says, "Most certainly in a commercial venture. However with St. Paul's being a blue-collar community a clause was written into the agreements stating, if a family did move away the contracts would-be non-binding. All of which brings us to the end of that year with most families having left Stockland."

With O'Daly's account coming to an end Sheri sits in disbelief, and then asks, "Weren't you at all suspicious as to why the community hadn't been repopulated?"

O'Daly repositions himself in the chair he's sitting in and says, "The Church was going through a change at that time, which had allowed a gentle breeze of renewal to take place. With that said we had many irons in the fire with little attention being paid to St. Paul's, or it's problems, consequently it fell through the cracks. However, some years later we learned that N.I.T. Property Assessment and Acquisition Inc., a subsidiary of

Pyxis International, was the one making the actual purchases, at double the market value per home. The rumor has it, N.I.T. was speculating on Delphi's need for additional real estate. Anyway, after the last transaction had taken place and there wasn't a structure left standing, we realized a decision had to be made on how the Church's property was to be handled. So we reluctantly came to the conclusion the buildings had to be demolished and we would have to leave. At that point, N.I.T. fenced off the boundaries of the former town, and walked away without any improvements being made, leaving me very suspicious as to what really had taken place. This entire affair was, and still is quite an embarrassment to the diocese."

Sheri realizes O'Daly was sincere in his account and now requires that he's to be more cooperative in the future, saying, "Listen John, it's important we work together. That means if you know something you're to share it with me no more holding back. It's obvious Burtrom's been affected by this, then we have a whole community that's been bought out. There's something going on, I'll find out what's happened but they'll have to be a few changes, first on the list, there's to be no more shell games. Farmsworth, Post, and Tom Waters are under my authority now, and you will be too. In short, I'm calling the shots." O'Daly needs to resolve this matter so he agrees to the terms, whereby lifting a burden that's been there for decades.

With the bidding of farewells Sheri and Alex leave the building and drive away in search of a convenience store that sells gasoline and sandwiches. After Sheri had stopped for fuel and eats they're en route once again now heading in the direction of the Latham Interchange, then onto 87 North. Sheri's already into his egg salad sandwich and decides he's had enough to eat and watches Alex unwrap his tuna delight. Then remarks, "I guess you're doing better than me, I've lost my appetite for some reason." Alex's all observing eye detects there's something wrong and asks, "You look a little peaked around the edges, is everything ok?" With his attitude now showing Sheri takes the next few minutes and explains the discussion he and O'Daly had.

Alex seems uneasy with the topic, and expresses his concern, "This whole situation appears to be bigger than both of us, we could be facing a giant. And from what I can see there's very few volunteers rallying around us for support."

With the stress gradually passing Sheri offers a little encouragement, saying, "You know, Rome wasn't built in a day, patience and resolve will have to be our allies."

The remaining half- hour drive is one of contemplation with each man reflecting on the events of that day leaving them committed to the completion of this project. O'Daly's confidence in these men would-be the driving force clearing a path to a better understanding of the situation.

As Alex and Sheri reach the Lodge they find Littea ready to leave, and with no more than a wave of her hand she's gone.

That evening as the moon reflections it's glow off the silken waters of the lake each man is left with some measure of enchantment whereby they're able to dismiss that day's misfortune. However during the night while secluded in his room Sheri lays in bed clearly agitated with the images of that day, and with no relief his mind wonders as to the whereabouts of Stockland's former residents. This anxiety lasts well into the late hours, and is finally broken as an unannounced thunderstorm presents itself. The rain beating on the windowpanes sweeps away the sounds of that day, while the flashes of lightning blots out the impressions firmly embedded in his mind.

Chapter Twelve

The following morning finds Sheri sleeping in, and Alex fabricating a makeshift bulletin board which will display yesterday's photos in their order of importance.

While Alex pins the last photo to the collage Sheri makes an unannounced visit. With eyes half- open he shuffles in holding a cup of coffee, then as he sips the brew it enables him to focus. With Sheri's perception more exact he says, "You certainly have my approval, well done."

Alex takes pride in his task and places the display on a nearby table, saying, "At least it'll demonstrate the dynamics of the situation."

With that being said Burtrom enters the room and walks toward the table and recognizes one of the pictures as the outline of the church's foundation, then he says, "The photos do record the devastation, but they say nothing as to why." Then the old man sits in a neighboring chair expressing wonder as he recalls, June weddings, beautiful brides, and elaborate ceremonies, all reminiscent of happier times. Now sitting alone he and the photographs keep one another company.

Sheri places his coffee cup down and says to Burtrom, "Your performance at St. Paul's had nothing to do with what went on in Stockland, those events were beyond your control. However we're still left with the Keno evaluation needing to be dismissed, and the Wallman report requiring our attention. Wallman is well disciplined and has the respect of his colleagues, all of which makes him more creditable."

Burtrom is concerned with his reputation and says, "I'd like to make some kind of contribution."

Sheri gives the proposal some thought, and then replies, "Maybe we should give that some consideration, you certainly have excellent organizational skills, all we have to do is --."
.
Alex interrupts the conversation, saying, "I've a thought, if that one picture stimulated his memory just think what the

others could do. We have to give Burtrom an opportunity to review these photographs. We have nothing to lose, and everything to gain."

Sheri gives a nod of approval then establishes the ground rules, saying, "Only on one condition, you're to keep detailed notes. Then when you're satisfied with those, try matching up the photos with one of the old travel maps in the files. We'll at least have a limited reconstruction of the community, and that's better than nothing."

As Burtrom sorts through the photographs Sheri and Alex start walking in the direction of the patio. Then removing the protective covers from the furniture Sheri positions his recliner facing Stone River. A tributary that supplies the current which produces the electrical power for the household, which in turn continues on into the lake thereby completing it's task. After Sheri is seated he says to Alex, "You know on the surface of things Burtrom's assignment may seem insignificant, however there's a fairly good chance he'll succeed, especially with the insight he has." Sheri gives Alex credit for the concept saying, "Your idea was brilliant. What prompted you to go in that direction?"

Alex is embarrassed by the attention, and says, "All the man needed was a little confidence. He's competent enough to look at pictures and the truth of the matter is we need all the help we can get, hopefully his recall will be accurate. Besides it'll occupy a good portion of his time allowing us to go in other directions."

Sheri is now free to focus his attention on other matters, saying, "We should rethink our objectives, there maybe other options we need to consider."

With the sunlight in his eyes Alex moves his chair underneath the cantilevered deck where there's more shade, and then replies, "I know what you're trying to say, and you're right. However if we forge ahead without exercising some kind of caution we very well could end up hip deep in alligators. Remember this odyssey started with a sick priest, now we have an entire community wiped off the map. All of which leaves me very suspicious, I think we better watch our topknots."

Sheri has displayed guarded optimism throughout this assignment. However with uncertainty looming his enthusiasm begins eroding, as he says, "I don't think anyone's going to lift our topknots, but at times I think we're in a maze, going in one direction and then another."

With Sheri needing reassurance Alex uses an analogy, which may help the process along, and says, "If a hunter isn't vigilant, he could very well lose his meal, let me explain. Suppose there's a hunt and no one's focussing on the signs, then they'll return empty handed, and that's what we have here. I'm fond of Burtrom but the emotional gauntlet he's running through has just enough room for one man. As for Stockland, I'm sure they were fine people however the destiny that's befallen them is now consummated. We have to live in the moment and deal with each problem as they present themselves. The pieces will come together, however you'll have to think about detaching, everyone marches to a different drummer even Burtrom. As they say, keep your eye on the ball."

Sheri now realizes that as a young fledgling is thrown from the nest Burtrom too must leave the security of his creative imagination, and accept the reality of his situation and that of his former parishioners.

With the cloud of uncertainty still lingering about both men return to the game room and resume their assessment of the material that had been inventoried. With the contents now stacked in front of each box, Sheri turns to Alex saying, "This is worse than I thought, it'll take forever to go through this stuff."

Alex walks over to the contents of the second box and begins to go through the material, then locates one particular file, saying, "The other day while I was trying to organize this mess I came across this." He hands the folder over to Sheri and patiently waits for a reply.

Sheri sits there in disbelief as he reads the document, then in astonishment, he exclaims, "If I'm interpreting this right they're medical bills for some two dozen families, including hospital bills from St. Joseph's in Albany, and everyone of them have been stamped paid in full!" Alex knowing the amount now kneels over the third stack of files and retrieves a set of financial books. Alex returns to his chair and selects one of the books, and fingers each page then abruptly stops to where the ledger reveals a notation regarding the renovation funds. He hands the book over to Sheri and he reviews the entries, saying, "Look at these dates, after three years of raising funds Burtrom uses the money to pay off medical bills. Man oh man, I'd like to see how he's going to explain this one!"

Sheri leans back in his chair, and asks, "Is there anything else I should know about?" Alex reaches for an envelope marked confidential, then he hands it over to Sheridan, who promptly opens the envelope and withdraws an authorization form for two rites of exorcism. Both of which had been approved by the diocese, and signed by John O'Daly.

As Sheri's face turns red Alex realizes there's a need to defuse the situation and asks, "What is it?" With no response he says, "We're in this together you might as well tell me."

Sheri agonizes over Alex's discovery, then out of necessity he finally says, "We have a very delicate situation calling for caution, and before taking any position I'll have to know the reason why Burtrom paid these bills. Then after I've dealt with that I'll have to challenge O'Daly's decision with regards to these exorcisms there could be a possible connection. In any event the Church has established a strict protocol for this ritual, mandating compliance!" Sheri is somewhat concerned with the latter issue and continues to say, "This rite is my forte and O'Daly is well aware of it!"

With the winds of discontent brewing up a storm, both men realize there has to be a break in the routine, so Alex says, "Listen, Buck's Roadhouse is having another Lumberman's Dinner this evening, all you can eat for eight dollars and ninety-five cents. We could turn the trip into an outing, and afterwards we might find we've developed a new perspective towards things."

Sheri is delighted with the idea leaving Alex feeling more comfortable with the situation they've been dealing with.

With arrangements completed for Burtrom's care both men walk down to the beach and set out in the Adirondack guide boat making their way along the shoreline to Buck's. The short thirty- minute row delivers this unlikely pair to shallower waters, enabling them to tie off at the slip, often referred to as Buck's port of call.

As the men leave the docking area they continue up the path and through a congested clientele who are eagerly competing in a festival of activities. After they enter the building Buck welcomes Alex in a cordial manner, saying, "There's my man, the place is a little crowded, please follow me." Thorton leads the men through the main dinning room, which proudly displays a double- faced fireplace, effectively heating the lounge and dinning area in the colder months. Now moving in the direction of an interior wall, a table with two place settings is readied for its intended guest. A gentle breeze now blows through an open window greeting the two men and offers them all the comfort one would desire. The next hour passes quite fast and takes their anticipation along with it, for the meal meets everyone's expectations, and in all of Sheri's culinary travels he's never been more delighted.

As Sheri and Alex are about to leave, Buck approaches their table, asking, "Did you boys enjoy your meal?"

Alex's reply is one of indifference, "It was alright." All the while knowing he received a good return for his money.

Buck is well aware of the difficulties these two men are faced with by way of a conversation he had with John Milner and says, "I know you boys are up against a brick wall, maybe you should cut bait on this one."

Then without notice Spike comes out of nowhere and begins staggering in Sheri's direction only to collapse just a few feet away from the table. Sheri, who at all times held this creature in contempt, begins to show compassion, saying, "He needs medical attention or something!"

Buck displays a wide grin, and then says, "I think we can rule out CPR." At which point he places three chairs around the animal.

As Thorton returns to the table Sheridan confront's him and the way the situation was handled by saying, "That's the best you can do?"

Bucks roars with laughter, then retorts, "I've done your something, that stupid thorn bush is drunk. He's been in John's beer most of the afternoon, and without needing a crystal ball I'll predict they'll be hell to pay in the Milner's household tonight.

There's only one thing that's worse than a porcupine with a hangover and that's John dragging his tail right along with spike's."

"Now lets put this little incident behind us shall we." At which point Buck motions to one of his waiters, and orders fresh blueberry pie and homemade ice cream for the three of them, hoping this gesture would make amends for Sikes behavior.

With the men finishing their dessert, Buck says, "For what it's worth, some years ago a group of semi- drivers reserved a room for a reunion of sorts. They had a grand old time swapping stories of equipment hauled, trips made, telling tales of road adventures. Well, if your observations are correct with regards to Stockland, then heavy equipment had to be delivered, and then operated, locate one of those drivers and you'll find your answers."

Alex asks, "Is their anyone specific we should be looking for?"

Alex and Sheri eagerly await a reply, then Thorton says, "As I recall the topic of discussion that evening was a driver by the name of Wesley Sumner, also known as the kid. He was young, but from all accounts a real natural. A fellow driver spoke of a return trip he made with Sumner and was mesmerized by

Wesley's talent. The story goes something like this, as they left the terminal Wesley had full control of a flat bed trailer loaded down with concrete blocks. Wes made such an impression, the other driver thought Sumner's performance had been choreographed. As the other fellow tells it Sumner was taking his commands off the tachometer, at which point, midway through a double-clutch he would shift the main transmission, then reach over and shift the auxiliary transmission three more times. Then there was an occasional split shift when both transmissions were shifted simultaneously, that my friends was something I'd liked to seen myself."

Sheri's attention is so focused on Buck's rendition that it's nearly eight o'clock before Alex is able to interrupt the tale, saying, "We have to be leaving its getting darker outside."

Thorton escorts the pair out of the dining room, and through Truckers' Row a passageway where photographs hang on the wall's honoring the patrons of yesteryear. Today the gallery draws more attention than usual, especially with Buck stopping halfway down the hallway saying, "Here's a picture of Wes standing alongside his tractor-trailer, look how that tanker shines. Anyway if I had to pick one person that might know something about Stockland it would- be the kid, and if he doesn't he'll find someone who does."

As the men return to the dock Alex exchanges parting waves with Thorton. Then turning to Sheri he says, "My intuition is telling me Bucks onto something."

As the two men push away from the mooring they seem engulfed in the darkness that now veils the lake. Alex uses the lights coming from within Londshadow's cabin as a heading while navigating North, then rowing Easterly he's finally able to recognize the Lodge as the moon reflects it's glow off the windowpanes.

After the men have secured the boat they return to the Lodge, where once again the game room welcomes them. Although physically tired each man seems physiologically refreshed, especially with Sheri viewing his task in a more pragmatic light. Sharing a nightcap with Hunter he realizes Thorton's idea had merit after all, and says to Alex, "I ignored Buck's suggestion as too simple, however after giving it some thought I've come to the conclusion he's right."

Alex is quick with a reply, saying, "I know he is, however when you get right down to it we'll be the one's looking for Sumner, and I haven't a clue how that's going to be accomplished."

Sheri looks up at the clock situated midway on the mantelpiece and says, "Neither do I, but there's one thing that seems certain, times running out."

Alex is about to call it a night, when he says, "We'll discuss the matter in the morning, but between now and then give some thought to those issues Burtrom has created. They're staring you down, and with the way our luck's been running it'll be a month of Sundays before we find Sumner."

With both men in agreement they secure the building and call it a night.

Chapter Thirteen

The following morning Sheri is in the kitchen pouring a cup of coffee when Burtrom enters the room seemingly refreshed, and says, "There's nothing like a good nights sleep and you know I actually experienced one last night."

Sheri is lost for words and looks on in astonishment, and then asks, "I've never seen you like this, what do you suppose is going on?"

Both men are relieved that Burns is finally getting some rest, then Burtrom says, "I've experienced so many health problems since my ordination, and with no one taking an interest as to the cause, I felt abandoned. However all that's changing, hopefully I'll be able to get this monkey off my back once and for all."

Sheri knows what's in store for the old man, and cautions him by saying, "Your opinion of what's been accomplished could be fleeting, we still have to find out what's wrong with you. In the meantime we'll eat breakfast, then discuss the matter afterwards."

Thirty minutes later they're off to the den with Sheri hoping he'll be able to accomplish the business at hand. He positions himself behind the desk while Burtrom takes a seat alongside of Alex's collage. As Sheri opens the folder marked medical cost he notices Burtrom displaying an indifferent look as he turns his head in the other direction. Sheri now opens the financial book that Alex had given him and begins his inquiry by saying, "It appears from these records the money you collected for the renovation project was used to offset the medical bills of these parishioners and with that said I'd like to understand why!"

Burtrom straightens up in his chair, and retorts, "What makes you think I owe you, or anyone else an explanation?"

Sheri immediately goes on the offensive by saying, "These figures paint a pretty accurate picture, and its telling me St.

Joseph's Hospital received a good portion of the money your parish raised!"

Burtrom feels awkward with this line of questioning, and says, "See here, I was a priest before you were born, and I'm entitled to a little more respect!" Burns can hardly compose himself as he continues, "Listen here, the Church happens to be it's people, and when they're in need we're expected to help them. Furthermore it was their money, and with that understood the parish council met and decided to help those individuals that needed it the most. Then, if there were any funds leftover it would-be used to restart the project."

Sheri knows he'll soon lose the argument to reason, and feels it's important to establish his position by saying, "You should had known better, a decision like that can only come from the bishop."

Burtrom had always held himself to the highest ethical standards, however those sentiments alone aren't enough, so he proceeds with an explanation, "It seemed every time I made an appointment with the Bishop's office it was cancelled, then rescheduled, only to be cancelled again! My people were suffering, and needed help. So as I've said before we were required to make some tough decisions, and moving the renovation project to the bottom of the list happened to be one of them. You of all people should realize the position I was in."

Sheri knows there's nothing left to the argument and now redirects his energy toward those questions that will leave him with a better understanding of the situation, "Wasn't there a policy in place whereby St. Joseph's was allowed to forgive debt that had been acquired by those less fortunate?"

Burtrom stares past Sheri and through the window, as if he were looking for the answers somewhere in the vastness of time and space. Then suddenly the thin cord attached to reality draws him back to the now and he replies, "We tried going that route, some families qualified, others didn't. Then there was the cost of medications, nothing at that time seemed real, but it was, and I have the receipts to prove it."

Both men sit in silence hoping a decree would-be proclaimed exonerating the other of any blame. Then with a need to move on, Sheri asks, "The files now reveal you applied for two exorcisms on behalf of certain individuals, can you tell me if these rites were carried out, and if so what lead to the decision?"

Burtrom displays a little more self-confidence, as he says, "Two families came to me under similar circumstances both seeking spiritual relief. So with the best of intentions I tried to help, however it was all in vain for neither of these individuals seemed to respond. So I turned the matter over to John O'Daly's office, whereupon arrangements were made for medical evaluations. The final report was somewhat vague, but did suggest each person may had used illicit drugs for recreational purposes, resulting in psychedelic imagery."

Sheri seems puzzled by the degree of insight Burtrom has acquired, and asks, "If you turned these cases over to O'Daly how did you learn about the medical evaluations?"

Burtrom replies, "Shortly after the examines were given I received a telephone call from John's office informing me of the results."

Sheri now wonders if his assignment with Burtrom was a diversion of sorts keeping him distracted long enough where he might recognize Stockland as a final chapter to his manuscript.

Burtrom is showing concern for Sheri as he's now displaying signs of confusion, and asks, "You appear disturbed by something, is everything all right?"

Sheri appears quite startled, then realizes the direction he must go, and presses on with one more question, "Would you or John know the name of the individual who did the examines?"

Burtrom leans forward as to pronounce a new revelation, but only a routine reply comes forth as he says, "As I remember John mentioned something about a nurse telephoning him with the results."

With both men knowing they've reached the end of their session Burtrom says, "David do both of us a favor, and telephone O'Daly's office, they're the ones with the answers."

Sheri realizes Burtrom is right and walks him to the door saying, "We've made enormous strides this morning, and with a little luck we'll accomplish even more."

With Burtrom now gone Sheri reviews the images enshrined in Alex's collage, and begins to feel powerless over the situation, then the telephone rings, it's Waters from O'Daly's office, saying, "Hello Sheri, Tom Waters. We've been served notice the hospital is going ahead with their inquiry, and you're expected to be in attendance."

With the Keno situation becoming an annoyance, Sheri says, "I'll be there, however I have a feeling their parade is going to be rained on." Sheridan calms down long enough to put the matter in perspective then continues to say, "Now that I have your attention, they're two questions that need answering. First, who on your end reviewed the Stockland exorcisms, and second, who was the doctor that took part in the evaluation?"

Waters has an interest in case histories such as this one and replies, "John O'Daly, and a devil's advocate argued both cases, with a decision being rendered by a canon lawyer from another dioceses. It was done that way because John wanted something more than a standard protocol. Now with regards to the evaluation, it's one of those gray area's where the Bishop will have to make the decision."

With his patience growing thin, Sheri asks, "Well, is he in?"

Waters places the call through to O'Daly, saying, "Bishop, David Sheridan is on line one." John welcomes the intrusion by saying, "Thank goodness, I've been rescued from this paper work, how can I be of help?"

Sheridan makes the same request as before, for the name of the medical practitioner who was involved in the Stockland evaluations. O'Daly is confident in Sheri's need to know and agrees to the review, then he instructs Waters to locate the files. Within minutes the sealed records are in his possession, John props the telephone receiver to his shoulder while he breaks the seal. Silence now dampens the moment, then in astonishment O'Daly exclaims, "You won't believe this, it's Keno!"

As this bureaucratic nightmare begins to unravel Sheri's frustration clearly shows, as he says, "Have you any idea how important these cases are? Then to top it off you mention nothing of your involvement in the handling of them!"

O'Daly seems confused as to the facts, then fumbles for an explanation, saying, "This is exactly why I enacted an expanded protocol, so there wouldn't be any slip-ups, and here I am the chief offender! In any event the proceedings had barely started when an emergency conference of Bishops was about to assemble in Washington. However before leaving I appointed a proxy on my behalf, that's why you see my name as presiding. It's still peculiar that Keno's name comes up twice in the same hour. What do you suppose is going on?"

The telephone line falls silent, then Sheri replies, "It maybe just a coincidence, but from where I'm sitting its simple math, one doctor who's missed diagnosed three individuals is equal to a pile of misery."

With his schedule backing up, O'Daly says, "We'll have to discuss this matter at a later date. However in the meantime you'll have to examine other possibilities the good Doctor hasn't considered, and if they stand-up to scientific and medical scrutiny we'll know he's out to lunch, and he'll be expected to pay the bill!"

As the telephone conversation comes to an end, Alex enters the room saying, "If that smile gets any wider you'll hurt yourself." Sheri then explains the dialogue he had with O'Daly nearly verbatim, and as he's about to finish, Hunter interrupts the narrative, saying, "Hold on my friend you're far too excited, let's take this one step at a time, and we'll start with that phrase you use, connecting the dots. Well, where's your next dot?"

Sheri's frustration begins to show as he says, "Damn it, I haven't a clue, furthermore we're dealing with ancient history, and I'm not an archaeologist!"

Alex is now in the process of reviewing the collage, when he says, "If I were to venture a guess I'd say a trucker like John Milner would know how we might locate Sumner."

With a game plan in place its decided they'd eat lunch and then visit John.

An hour later both men begin walking in the direction of the Milner's homestead. And with only a few hundred yards behind them Sheri wonders if Alex had seen something in the collage earlier in the day, "I was watching you going over the photographs this morning, and was wondering if you noticed anything?"

Alex glances in Sheri's direction, and says, "I had an opportunity to step back and reflect on those images, then realized I needed to interpret them. Well, we saw what everyone else sees, nothing, with a chain-link fence surrounding it, and that's a helluva expense to keep people away from nothing. Then there was an operational cost for equipment, man- hours and disposal fees for the rubble. That in itself makes me more than a little suspicious."

As they leave the trail that had escorted them through the woods the men reenter Portage Road, thereby shortening their trip by ten minutes. They're now in view of the Milner's home, and Littea, who is tending a nearby garden. Sheri now becomes concerned, saying, "You know Littea and surprises, she's apt to go up one side of us and down the other."

Alex picks up his stride, and says, "Don't worry, I have a feeling after yesterday's outing we'll be better company than John or Spike."

Littea who's been kneeling in her flowerbed looks up in astonishment as the men draw closer and then says, "Look who's here, Pete and Repeat!" Both men seem offended by the sarcastic greeting and look to one another as if to say, poor timing. Littea then realizes she's developed a poor attitude and apologizes, "Sorry fellows, just because my day is ruined doesn't mean yours has to be. I need to be more hospitable, especially when visitors are few and far between." She picks up her gardening tools, and straightens up in the direction of John's tractor-trailer, and says, "Maybe that truck is the reason people stay away, it's an eyesore and stinks when John fires it up." The tension now eases as Littea breaks into an inviting smile, saying, "Come on in, we'll have coffee and you boys can tell me why you're here."

As they walk up the stairs and onto the front porch Sheri realizes this way of life had a certain appeal he missed years earlier.

While Littea is preparing to serve her guest, she says, "If you fellows think I'm going to watch Burtrom again you're mistaken!"

Alex holds his freshly poured cup of coffee and then says, "No, nothing like that, we thought John might be around, we have a few questions that need answers. You see last evening

197

Buck suggested we locate a trucker by the name of Wesley Sumner, hoping he might know something about Stockland."

Sheri interrupts the conversation, saying, "The truth of the matter is we need all the help we can get."

Littea cocks her head to one side and begins fingering her braided hair, saying, "I doubt if John ever heard of Sumner." Then with a puzzling look, she asks, "Are you boys sure Buck didn't mention my name?" Alex and Sheri both shake their heads no. Littea seems embarrassed, however continues on to say, "It was nearly twenty-five years ago, well before I ever heard of John Milner, that a group of us, mostly in our late teens would visit Owl's Head Lake just North from where we are now. With the two lakes only being separated by a strip of land a quarter of mile wide we would make the portage then paddle our canoes around visiting friends. Anyway that particular summer the Sumner's moved into the area from Albany and established a summer residence along the shoreline. Later on Wes and I became friends and dated throughout his college years. Then, after graduating with a degree in journalism Wesley became disenchanted with the job offers coming in, and decided to follow his instincts. At that point our relationship began to deteriorate, we did talk about marriage, but under the circumstances neither one of us knew what we wanted so we decided to wait."

Littea's eyes begin to gloss over with tears, which eventually find their way onto her cheek only to be swept away with the back of her hand. Then she continues to say, "He did find work driving tractor - trailer for a firm outside of Albany, they actually brought him up through the ranks. Wes had real talent, you could say he was bitten by the bug, and he knew it. The only time that man was truly happy was when those eighteen wheels were rolling and he could shift another gear. That's when I decided to end the relationship."

Sheri seems confused as to the facts and looks for an explanation saying, "You married John and he's a trucker what's the difference?"

Littea pours another cup of coffee for herself then sits down, and explains, "Wesley would -be gone for weeks at a time, John on the other hand is home just about every night. Maybe once or twice a year he'll layover due to weather conditions."

With Littea speaking in the past tense Alex begins wondering if Wesley will ever be found, and then he asks, "Have you heard anything as to Wesley's whereabouts?"

Littea is now confronted with her emotional attachment to Sumner and begins to sob, its only after composing herself once again is she able to continue, "One day last summer while making my usual trip to Oak's Trading Post, I saw Wesley's father standing in line at the checkout. We engaged in idle chitchat for a while, then he informs me Wesley was no longer trucking, and was living in New York City somewhere between the Bowery and Central Park, depending upon the time of year. It was obvious at that point neither of us could add anything more to the conversation so we parted company."

Both men realize they've reached the end of their inquiry, and with an air of stillness now bringing closure to the conversation Alex and Sheri thank Littea for her help, and begin to leave.

Littea bounces to her feet, saying, "Are you boys still interested in finding Wesley?"

Alex seems uncertain in his response, and turns to Sheri who says, "Only if we have a chance."

Littea rushes into her sewing room and returns with a photograph of Wesley, "You'll need a picture, it's a little old, however I'm certain it'll be of some help." With a smile and a flicker of hope she hands it over, saying, "At some point I'd like the photo back, it, and the memories are all I have left."

Sheri takes possession of the photo then the two men begin walking along the path which will eventually lead them through West Woods, and finally back to the retreat.

That evening while sitting on the rear patio both men practice the art of stargazing, with Sheri asking Alex, "Why do you spend so much time outside?"

Alex now points to a shooting star, then offers a reply to Sheri's question, saying, "It's the winter months, they're cold and long with very little sunlight. So when we have nicer whether I'm outside as much as possible."

Alex continues the discussion by recalling Littea's relationship with Wesley saying, "Her account of Wesley is believable right up to the point where she meets his father. I'm not saying it didn't happen, with certainty it had, my concern is how could a bright guy like Sumner ended up this way?"

Sheri's been harboring those very sentiments, and picks up the conversation, saying, "That's what we have to find out, I wasn't figuring on another problem, however if it means things will move along a little faster I really don't mind. The only thing that'll slow us down is finding him, New York City covers a lot of territory not to mention its population."

With a chill in the air Alex and Sheri return to the warmth of the Lodge and decide to call it a night.

Chapter Fourteen

Friday morning ushers in a chill, reminiscent of a summer season that's already in decline. With this being the first of August the Adirondack Mountain's are beginning to show signs of longer shadows, leaving one's imagination open to the colder months laying ahead. Now, in the comfort of a warm kitchen Sheri is midway through breakfast when he hears Littea walking through the rear entryway, saying, "I trust everyone's well."

With an uninterrupted nights sleep yielding no clue as to how Wesley could be found, Sheri's about to give a negative report when the telephone rings. With coffee cup in hand he walks into the den, and grabs the receiver, saying, "Hello."

"Good morning Sheri."

He recognizes the voice as that of Richard Post, and replies, "Good morning Dick, how can I be of help?"

Richard is all business as he says, "Sheri I need an affidavit from you explaining your position on Burtrom's unauthorized discharge."

With his reputation now being called into question Sheri places the conversation on hold just long enough to process an idea or two, then asks, "Richard, do you have any contacts with the N.Y.C.P.D.?"

Richard assumes a defensive posture by asking, "What does that have to do with the affidavit?"

Sheri then says, "I'll have the affidavit prepared by tomorrow, however there's a catch, you'll have to pick it up, and in return I'll be asking a favor." With little choice in the matter Richard agrees to the terms, leaving Sheri with one final task, convincing Post that his help is necessary if they're to find Sumner.

That afternoon and evening are spent in drafting, and finalizing the document, making sure every medical judgement he had made was based on sound scientific principles recognized within the medical community.

However that night Sheri begins to experience doubt in his medical decision whereby he's left second -guessing his disciplines leaving him with only a few hours sleep.

At first light the sun begins radiating it's warmth not only on the new day, but also on Sheri depressed spirit enabling him to display the courage needed to defend his position. With that being said he drives over to Karl Middleton's office, where Karl's wife Carol notarizes the document.

As Sheri returns from Middleton's office he drives into the Lodge's parking lot and notices Richard along with Alex casting dry lines. He looks on as the event continues, and fears if something is said it would break their concentration. Then Dick exercises a perfect cast into an open area alongside the west-end of the building. He hits his target and exclaims, "That's the way it's done." Alex has been less fortunate, and now sits in frustration untangling his line from a misguided cast.

Sheri approaches the two would-be anglers exclaiming, "Ok boys, fun and games are over, at least for the time being, we have to get down to business!" They grab their fishing gear and proceed to follow Sheri around back of the building and onto the patio. He then points to their respective seating arrangements and hands the affidavit over to Post saying, "This satisfies my end of our agreement, as for yours, that's a little more problematic. You see we need help locating a chap by the name of Wesley Sumner."

Richard is surprised by the request because Sheridan knows his department has limitations and then he says, "Do you think for one minute I'm going to exhaust my limited resources looking for someone I don't even know!" Then in a moment of enlightenment he exclaims, "Ah, I see where this is going, that's why you asked about my connections with the N.Y.C.P.D.!"

Sheri now realizes he's kept Richard in the dark far too long and apologies by saying, "I'm sorry Dick, this is all my fault. I should had explained earlier, this man could be the key to our understanding of Burtrom, and why Stockland had been razed."

Alex watches as the embarrassment fades from Sheri's face. Then hints to Sumner's whereabouts, saying, "Littea mentioned she had spoke with Wesley's father a year ago, and he told her Wes was living in New York City, somewhere between the Bowery and Central Park."

Richard sits up in his chair, and says, "Stop right there, I think I'm getting the picture, you're trying to tell me he's living on the street!"

Sheri's voice is barely audible, as he replies, "Yah, the street."

With nothing more to be said, both men avoid eye contact with Richard hoping they would escape ridicule. Then Richard sees the situation as being hopeless, and yields to their request, saying, "You win, I can't sit around here arguing all day and expect to fish too. However, with regard to your boy in the city, don't expect tangible results any time soon, this search is low on the priority list. These officers are the finest, but there's a limit to what they can do. It's a big city with a lot of people, and some feel quite comfortable being lost in the crowd. Anyway, I'll pull a few strings and we'll see what comes up. I just hope it's worth the effort."

Sheri remembers Littea's outdated photograph of Wesley and hands it over to Richard, saying, "This should be of some use. If you're willing to have a few copies made, I'll be able to return the original. Littea has developed an attachment to both the memories, and the picture."

Richard nods in a sympathetic fashion, then turns to Alex, saying, "My man, let's tie flies and throw line, I've a feeling we're going to catch fish." Alex displays unbridled enthusiasm as he leads Dick off the patio and into the den where they spend the afternoon tying flies hoping to make use of them later that day.

Sheri remains behind reflecting on all the uncertainties, including Burtrom's recovery, and Sumner's whereabouts along with his level of cooperation if he's ever found. Then there's the on going mystery of Stockland, and its demise.

Later that evening, Richard finally informs Sheri the affidavit was only a precautionary measure. The inquiry into his unauthorized discharge of Burns had been put on hold. O'Daly's attorneys had advised John, his agent, meaning Sheri had full authority to act on his behalf. With the situation now in their camp John patiently waits for Sheri's final report before putting permanent closure to Burtrom's problems, Keno's behavior, or to the anticipated need's of the former residents of Stockland.

The following morning after everyone had finished breakfast Richard excuses himself, saying, "Sorry boys I'll have to leave, it's a long drive back. In any event it's been nice seeing all of you again, and Alex I'd be proud to accept anyone of those fly's we talked about." Then looking at Sheri he asks, "Do you mind walking me to the car?" With no objections being made the two men leave the building.

As they approach the parking lot, Richard asks, "I know we haven't discussed this, but have you given any thought to where Sumner will stay after he's found?"

Sheri realizes he's been shortsighted, and hasn't given the matter enough thought, and says, "They'll be plenty of time to figure that one out, first we'll have to find him."

With the conversation now ending Richard drives away leaving Sheri standing in the morning sunlight somewhat apprehensive as to the outcome of this exercise.

Alex watches the car leave from the front porch then walks down into the parking lot, and asks, "Is everything ok?"

Sheri seems startled, as he replies, "Damn it, you shouldn't sneak around like that!"

Alex's concern seems justified as he says, "I wasn't, you're the one who was lost in time and space."

As both men begin their walk back to the Lodge, Sheri explains, "You're right, I was lost and still am for words. As I watched Richard driving away I felt as if our last vestiges of hope had left. I was so confident all we had to do was connect the dots. Now with the canvas riddled with them I have no way of knowing what kind of picture is emerging."

Alex offers a smile, along with a few words of comfort, saying, "I detect a little ego deflation and you know that's not a bad thing, it keeps us right sized so our hats will fit. Admittedly this situation will involve time, remember the old adage hurry up and wait, well brother start rocking, because nothing going to change until Sumner is found." With a smile coming from each man the tension begins to fade, leaving Sheri wondering how long he'll be benched.

As Alex and Sheri go about with their daily routine Burtrom tries to understand Sumner and the role he'll play in all this. Then that evening while passing Sheri in the upstairs hallway, he says, "You know there's no reason why this Sumner fellow has to be involved, he can't possible contribute anything to this situation. If you ask me tracking him down is a big waste of time!"

Sheri senses that Burtrom is no longer feeling he's the center of attention, and says, "Burt neither one of us has the answers, and to be honest with you we can use all the help that's out there. In the meantime get some sleep, things will look differentially in the morning."

With Burtrom now reassured, Sheri continues on down the hallway and into his room.

Chapter Fifteen

It's now the 28th of November, a foreboding month of sorts casting its shadow not only on the isolated days ahead, but on the three men as well, commanding each to his daily duties. One such task is storing the Camero away for the winter in John Milner's barn, thereby protecting Sheri's treasure from the colder elements. With flurries just around the corner he's made arrangements for the use of John's pick-up truck on those special occasions when transportation was needed.

Alex on the other hand doesn't need motivation. He's well aware of what's to come, and has furnished the Lodge with an adequate supply of firewood, and oil for the lamps. Then he and Sheri installed the storm windows, and cleaned all three chimneys. With there chores now completed everyone is assured of a comfortable winter.

Last on the list would-be Burtrom's contribution, which by all accounts has stopped, and has been replaced by clinical depression, manifesting itself with classical signs, such as insomnia, and a loss in appetite. All of which is being observed under Sheri's watch, and is soon corrected with an adjustment in Burtrom's medication.

Later in the morning Sheri takes time to review the files, once again hoping to find some connection between Burtrom's illness and those of his former parishioners. However as the hour's pass he takes on the appearance of a defeated man and with little insight he becomes overpowered with despair and entertains the thought of resigning. Then without notice the silence is broken with an unsettling ring coming from the telephone. Sheri is startled by the sound then he lifts the receiver and says, "Hello."

The voice on the other end of the line is that of Richard Post saying, "Sheri, I have good news, we've found your man."

Sheri is tongue-tied and it's only after he exercises a little self-control is he able to say, "That's wonderful, how's Wesley doing?"

Richard then replies, "Not well I'm afraid, he's penniless and living in a mission house where he's drying out."

Sheri's impatience begins to show as he says, "That's the best you can do?"

Sheridan had crossed the line and Post has had just about enough of his attitude, and replies, "You have some nerve, while you've been sitting on your ass we've been the one's looking for this guy!"

With Sheri in his rightful place Richard continues to say, "Now that we have an understanding I'll finish what I was trying to say. Yesterday as one of my contacts was delivering supplies to a mission house he noticed Sumner from one of the pictures we circulated. The rest is history, the officer notified me, and I in turn spoke with Wesley explaining the circumstances, at which point he agreed to help. Listen, from what I've been told this guy's in rough shape, and I'm not one to dash anyone's hopes, but this could be a lost cause."

After the briefing Sheri is prepared to drive into the city, saying, "Richard just give me the directions to the mission, and I'll pick him up myself."

Richard knows Sheridan is far too excited, and says, "Relax, there's no need to pop your cork again. He's already left the city, the officer is driving Wesley as far as St. Jonathan's, then Farmsworth will take the second leg to Birch. So, if everything goes as planned you'll have guests this evening."

With the conversation ending Sheri rushes into the game room displaying unbridled enthusiasm, saying, "Alex, they've found Wesley, he and Farmsworth will be here tonight!"

As the fireplace offers its comfort to the room, so does the news of Sumner's return thereby ending a discontentment that's lasted for nearly four months. New life emerges, giving the trio a reason to celebrate.

With accommodations having to be made Sheri and Burns press into service and prepare two additional rooms, while Alex shops at the trading post for additional supplies.

With the preparations almost completed Sheri calls Alex into the Kitchen where he warms up a quart of cider, and says, "I've been thinking about Wesley and the challenges he faced while living on the streets of New York. And realized he'll probably experience a few more difficulties while making the transition back to his former life style. Those unknowns worry me. It'll take a great deal of effort on everyone's part if he's to succeed."

Alex has always lived in the Lake Region, and yields a puzzling look as Sheri explains, "People living on the street do what they can to acquire what little possessions they have, which then necessitates a shopping cart existence. Whatever they own is taken from one place to another, they're very possessive, and suspicious by nature. No one can fault them, or their ways, it's a hard life with few breaks, and when they do come around it's usually in the form of broken promises."

Both men sit in silence, then Alex asks, "Have you any idea how we'll handle the situation?"

Sheridan replies, "We'll have to demonstrate our confidence in his ability to adjust, and the only way I can see that happening is by giving him free rein of the place, beyond that we'll handle each situation as they develop."

That evening as the hours exhaust themselves Sheri and Alex fall asleep in their chairs, leaving Burtrom alone in his room.

Then without notice the clock sitting midway on the mantelpiece strikes the hour and awakens both men, with Alex saying, "It's already ten o'clock, do you suppose something has happened?"

Sheri glances up at the timepiece and watches a light being reflected off the dial, and realizes it's coming from the headlights of a car. Then both men walk over to the bay window where they see a sedan pulling into the parking lot, then Sheri says, "It's Farmsworth with our guest."

Both men watch from the window as Brian helps Sumner out of the passenger seat. With one hand Farmsworth balances Wesley, and with the other he places a medium size canvas bag over his right shoulder. As they make their way onto the front porch Sheri relieves Brian of the bag. Exhausted from the trip Farmsworth expresses his gratitude as they enter the building with him saying, "Thanks, that's the last straw on this camels back. Listen I don't want to sound as if I'm insensitive, but what are your plans for this guy?"

Alex offers a helping hand and carries the bag in the direction of the staircase while Brian leads Wesley to his room, and within ten minutes their guest is settled in. Alex and Brian return to the first floor and find Sheri waiting in the game room, where he asks, "Is our prodigal son tucked in?"

Brian walks past Sheri and sits in a wingback chair situated next to the fireplace, and gazes into the embers, then leans closer to the heat in an attempt to warm his hands. With nothing being said Alex carefully places two more logs on the irons while Sheri patiently waits for a report. Then Farmsworth suddenly straightens up in a matter of fact way, and says, "Well we made it, I should say Wes has, he's asleep. You should had seen him, within minutes of his head hitting the pillow he was out." Brian develops a sense of satisfaction in knowing he's carried out Richard's directives and now leans back in his chair saying, "Today I found out how hard it really is to follow orders."

Sheri looks over at Brian, then says, "I have a pretty good idea, I've been sitting around here for nearly four mouths waiting for something to happen! Anyway that's my story, tell me about your trip."

With both men listening Brian embellishes his account of that afternoons activities, saying, "I received a telephone call from Richard around three o'clock this afternoon instructing me to meet with him immediately. Once I arrived at his office I was able to size-up the situation leaving me with only one option, pulling Dick aside and informing him of Sumner's need to bath, and if there were any objections he'd be the one driving Sumner to the Lodge." Brian always enjoyed protracting a story as long as he remained the center of attention, however this time

Sheridan patience is wearing thin as Farmswoth continues with his tale, "You should of been there. Within five minutes Dick had two security guards escorting Wesley to a nearby shower room thereby affording us an opportunity to rummage through his plastic bags. Well, to make a long story short we explained to Sumner the need to discard their contents, and with his permission we achieved that goal, it was pretty bad. Afterwards he and I walked downstairs to the lost and found department where we selected his new wardrobe, and then packed those items along with a few of his personal effects in an old duffel bag, and three hours later we're here. Look fellows it's been a long day and I need to rest, we can discuss Mr. Sumner and how I can of help in the morning." With that said, Farmsworth walks upstairs to his room, leaving Alex and Sheri wondering if he'd be of any real help.

With Brian out of the room Sheri says, "You know Alex, I'm afraid he'll end up crippled if he continues patting himself on the back that way." Both men smile as Sheridan continues, "I really feel sorry for that man, he hasn't a clue as to what's going on. I on the other hand have a feeling there's an experience of a lifetime just around the corner, and I wouldn't miss it for anything." With that said each man calls it a night.

Chapter Sixteen

The following morning Littea takes a few minutes out of her schedule to visit with Wesley, then after breakfast she goes about her duties. Wes on the other hand is in need of orientation, and turns to Sheri for help. Arrangements are then made where Alex and Farmsworth would spend the next three days familiarizing Wesley with his new environment, thereby making the transition a little more comfortable.

That weekend passes far too quickly, its Sunday evening now with everyone seemingly exhausted. Burtrom and Wes are already asleep in their rooms with Sheri and Alex playing cards in the game room. At which point Brian walks in and interrupts the game saying, "I hope you boys know what you're getting into, I've been listening to Sumner and he's in no position to answer any of your question, now, or any time in the future. He has only one concern, surviving the winter, and you gentlemen have helped him in accomplishing that feat!"

Sheri takes issue with Farmswoth statement, saying, "Brian you're a cynical son of a bitch. You've never taken the time to observe Wesley, I have, and noticed they're similarities between him and Burns!" Sheri watches as Farmsworth postures for a response and stops him in the attempt by saying, "Don't say a damn word, I know exactly what you're thinking, and it has nothing to do with Keno's diagnosis!"

Farmsworth defends his position, saying, "Wake up and smell the coffee, it's over, you're going into winter with two guys already in their own wonderland!"

Sheri knows Brian is right, but places more importance on a solution, saying, "Brian you have a point, however there's something so obvious about this situation, and we're missing it. Anyway if this matter goes unattended these guys will be lost between the cracks again, and we'll never know what's been going on."

With Brian's self-esteem still intact he displays a robust smile, and says, "You know me I'm always ready to lend a hand. As for the moment there's nothing more I can do here, so

I'll be leaving in the morning and it'll be you and Alex pulling the load once again." As Brian is about to leave the room he remembers a message O'Daly had left, and says, "John telephoned while you were out yesterday, and asked if you wouldn't mind visiting Longshadow. It has something to do with resolving their issue before Christmas. Well, I better get a few hours sleep, five o'clock is just around the corner."

The following days were somewhat of a psychological shakedown for Sumner, this is the first time since leaving the Lake Region he's been compelled to evaluate his former career, and the impact it's had on his life.

It's now Wednesday morning and Sheri is kept busy reviewing several documents in the den when halfway through the process Wesley enters the room and begins examining the fishing tackle that's displayed along the wall. Then, after a few minutes of silence Sumner says, "I suppose there's something to say about the simple things in life."

Sheri's been waiting for such an occasion, knowing all too well Wesley would open up if an opportunity presented itself. He puts the paper work aside, and replies, "You're right, and one of those things happens to be an old fashion conversation, so if there's something you want to talk about I'm willing to listen."

Wesley returns the pole to its place alongside the vintage collection, then sits down in a nearby chair, saying, "I've only been here six days and my whole life has been turned upside down. It's hard to make sense out of anything. While I was living on the street I was able to cope with situations and the people that created them. However all of that has changed, now all I can focus on is my lost identity and the opportunities that went along with it. In the scheme of things I do know where I've been, but what I don't understand is how I got there. And that really bothers me, leaving me wondering if I'll ever make the adjustment back into society. It's not easy walking that thin line, there some days I'm so feed up with this place I'd like to pack up and leave. Then on others the solace of the Lodge and the serenity of the mountains seem to call out that I'm to stay, leaving me with a sense of peace I haven't known in years."

Sheri looks into Wesley's eyes and sees a hollowness he's never seen in a man before and not knowing how to respond he makes an attempt at reassuring Sumner, saying, "You'll always have the promise of a new day, and the hope that comes with it. In the meantime we'll have to address your health issues, then we'll deal with the other problems later on."

With both men having a better understanding of the situation they now sit in the comfort of the den in an idle conversation hoping they'll get to know one another better. That is until Sheri recognizes the date that's been circled on the calendar, and realizes he must visit Longshadow. Sheri chooses his words carefully as not to alienate Sumner, then resorts to a tactful retreat saying, "These types of situations take time to resolve and when they do you'll be a better person for going through the experience, and remember I'll always be here if you need help. In the meantime I'm to run an errand for Bishop O'Daly, and if it's not done today he'll have my butt in a sling." Sumner feels more comfortable with the matter and agrees their discussion could be taken up again at a later date.

While Sheri gathers the paper work from the desk, Wesley leaves the security of the den and explores the shoreline, hoping to regain some degree of serenity. With the files now back in their respective folders Sheridan telephones John Milner requesting the use of his pick-up truck, while explaining the need to meet with Longshadow. John understands the importance of the mission and agrees to drop by with the truck.

With an unexpected case of cabin fever having developed Sheri can't wait to put distance between himself and the Lodge hoping the trip would-be a remedy for those unsettling feelings he's been experiencing. Now free from Burtrom and his care Sheri settles down and dismisses the anxiety that's been plaguing him since the onset of colder weather. With only a quarter of a mile to travel the ride becomes unbearable.

Drainage ditches alongside the road had never been considered in its construction thereby creating a washboard effect, requiring Sheri to use extreme caution while navigating around the potholes.

He's minutes of his destination and now recognizes the familiar smell of a wood fire, and begins reviewing a few last-minute thoughts. Then as he drives alongside the cabin the sound of truck tires passing over broken tree branches can be heard thereby alerting Longshadow. Moments later the old man rushes outside saying, "You'll never make it as a hunter you make too much noise."

Both men laugh and then escort one another inside the building and they spend the next two and half-hours occupied in a harmonious fellowship. Longshadow speaks fondly of his people and their oral history telling Sheri how their joys and suffering had sustained him through the years. Sheri then reciprocates with tales of his youth and the trials his grandparents endured while living in Ireland, and then again in this country. This quiet time seems to have bonded both men into a brotherhood of sorts, leaving each in respect of the other's hardships.

With the visit reaching its conclusion Longshadow excuses himself from their conversation and retrieves the signed copy of

O'Daly's document. He hands the agreement over to Sheri saying, "This very day after placing my signature to this paper, I fell asleep only to realize the spirit of creation had visited me in a vision. I saw you standing near the spot where the aircraft once landed many years ago. You looked on as the creator brought mankind into being, then with his nostrils flaring this new creation walked in the direction of an abundant life, only to be stopped by a sinister creature cloaked in a mist." Longshadow pauses long enough to collect his thoughts, then continues on to say, "Then an eagle of immense size flew over the landscape watching things I could barely see, that's when I awoke."

Longshadow now begins to show signs of confusion so Sheri politely thanks the old man for his preemptive awareness, and with a pleasant afternoon shared by both men, they bid the other farewell and Sheri drives away satisfied his task had been completed.

The return trip is uneventful, so much so Sheri remembers very little of the journey, simply because his attention had been focused on Longshadow and the events portrayed in his vision.

Sheridan now parks the pick- up truck in the Milner's driveway, and walks back to the Lodge where he goes directly to the den and resumes the task of reviewing files. Sometime later Alex enters the room, asking, "How did things go with Longshadow?"

Sheri responds to the question as if he's still looking for an answer, saying, "The afternoon was quite enjoyable. However when it came time to leave your grandfather spoke of a vision he had which in the end left both of us confused." Then Sheri continues with a methodical account of the afternoon's activities and concludes by saying, "I was really enjoying myself. Then your grandfather informs me of the nature of the vision saying I was standing near the old airfield watching how man became a living being, then some form of creature beset mankind. Anyway while all this was going on a giant eagle was circling in the air watching the events as they unfolded, leaving Longshadow somewhat frustrated as to what he couldn't see, and that's when he woke up."

Alex's reply is one of disbelief as he says, "He's always exhibited a strong character, and never displayed anything but sound judgment. The only thing that would explain this behavior would-be years of solitude, I suppose living alone has finally taken its toll."

Sheri directs his attention away from the files, and says, "This whole business is having an effect on me. All I had to do was pick-up the document. Instead my life's been complicated once again by another riddle with no apparent explanation."

Alex notices the fatigued expression on Sheri's face and offers an interpretation, saying, "Remember your science, dreams have their origins within the brain during R.E.M., that's the way man deals with mental activity. Listen, my grandfather is an old man looking for recognition in his later years. He wants to recapture those earlier times when he felt important and had something to contribute to his people. Let the issue go and in the meantime catch-up on a little sleep, then, after supper, if you still feel the need we'll discuss the matter further."

With a need to rest Sheri takes Alex's advice and napes for about an hour, then finishes a light supper and joins him in the Great Room. With both men now comfortably seated before the fireplace they engage in small talk for about thirty minutes, then Alex finally asks, "When are we getting around to Sumner, and what he knows about Stockland?"

Wesley's arrival had been somewhat of a distraction, however things are settling down now, and Sheri is beginning to wonder what Wesley really knows about Stockland. Then he says, "There's no time like the present, how about tomorrow morning around ten o'clock?" With each man in agreement Sheri continues to say, "The game room and den are cluttered with too many documents, we'll have to use this room, it's spacious enough where he'll feel comfortable. Anyway with him being the only game in town we want front row seats." Then a sense of the unknown captures the moment as Sheri expresses his concern, saying, "You know we have a very delicate situation, and with no way of knowing what the questions are we'll have no idea how he'll react."

Alex replies with a smile and says, "We experienced the same situation with Burtrom and everything turned out alright. There's no reason to think Sumner is any different. Now with regards to Longshadow's vision, are you able to put that behind you?"

Sheri gives the question some thought, then replies, "I personally can't accept your interpretation, because I feel the man believes what he says. In any event we'll have to wait this one out, and who's to say what providence has in store. With that said, we better get some sleep if we're to meet with Sumner in the morning."

Thursday morning makes it's arrival with a light dusting of snow and Sheri makes his by preparing breakfast, while Alex keeps busy restocking wood supplies alongside each of the three fireplaces. Now with breakfast and morning chores out of the way Sheri and Alex escort Wesley into the Great Room where Sheri says, "Wesley we've invited you to join us this morning hoping you could shed some light on the circumstances behind Stockland's demise. Thereby enabling us to develop a better understanding of the situation. To start with we need to learn as much as we can about the town and its people."

Although Wesley owned a home in Stockland most of his time was spent away on the road driving and resting in the sleeping compartment of his truck. However he does offer a superficial description of his experiences, saying, "I first became interested in Stockland while working for the Tri- State Transportation Company. At that point in my life I wanted to move closer to the Albany area, Stockland seemed convenient, I felt comfortable with the surroundings, and the commute was reasonable. All of which left me with the impression it would-be the right choice and it was. I enjoyed my work even though it kept me away for days, and even weeks. I really had the best of both worlds, a job I was happy with, and a modest bungalow that performed its duties as a sanctum providing me with all the comfort anyone could ask for."

Wesley's account suddenly yields to silence, as if he's recalling those earlier days, then Sheri interrupts that tranquillity by asking, "Did you notice anything unusual about the town?"

229

Sumner looks up in an attempt to collect his thoughts, and then says, "No, not at first, things appeared quite normal with everyone going about doing this or that. Then something strange began to happen over the next two years, every so often after returning from a road trip I would notice another home or two vacant. At first it didn't bother me, but after the second year I started to worry about the value of my property. Then a company known as N. I. T. Property Assessment and Acquisition approached me with an offer for my home, saying they wanted to develop the surrounding area into a resort community. So with a chance to double my money I accepted their offer and sold out."

Alex agitates the situation, by asking, "Weren't you at all suspicious as to their motive? None of that land has potential for that kind of development!"

Sumner defends his position by saying, "Stop acting like a damn know-it-all, I didn't have the answers then, and I certainly haven't a clue to what's going on with that situation now!" Sumner's words echo off the walls of the Great Room. Then after a moment of silence he says, "Anyway I accepted their offer and began the relocation process. It was a very difficult time in my life, I felt as if I had compromised my values by selling the property, and talking about it isn't helping." Choked up with emotion Wesley continues by saying, "Then my job with the trucking company underwent a change. Instead of long hauls I found myself being assigned to the equipment division hauling bulldozers, excavating equipment, and front- end loaders into the Stockland area for the sole purpose of razing the town. All of which left me feeling very uncomfortable!"

Sheri's seems to have developed some insight into the matter and says, "Relax Wes, we all know what happened. What we don't know is why, and as with most situations like this the plans and decisions are well thought out behind the closed doors of some board room."

Alex and Wesley sit there displaying a puzzling look then Sheri offers an explanation, saying, "Listen, this entire scheme is far too elaborate for only one person to have dreamed up. There has to be other players with separate agendas, along with their own set of rules." Sheri now turns to Wesley, and asks, "What happened after you delivered the equipment into the area?"

Wesley hears the words but the meaning is lost. He's a retiring individual and feels quite uncomfortable being at the focal point of their discussion. Alex finally encourages Sumner to continue whereby Wesley is able to say, "After I hauled the equipment and fencing material into the area a contractor showed up to do the work. While all that was going on I was

231

reassigned to transport duty, spending another two years hauling gasoline, and J.P.-4. Then, somewhere along the way the company felt I had a problem with liquor. I began to wonder myself because I had developed a low tolerance for the stuff. I feel uncomfortable talking about this matter because I have no way of knowing when that line was crossed, or why. Anyway the company felt my services were no longer needed, and the rest is history."

With Sumner's self-esteem somewhat deflated Sheri realizes it's time for a break and suggests they resume the discussion after lunch.

An hour later it's down to business with the three men joining Burtrom who's already in the den arranging the photographs in their order of importance. Then Sheri approaches the old man asking, "Have you been successful in identifying any other distinguishable features?"

Burns is frustrated with the task and replies with a scornful frown. Sheri feels a definite chill in the air and redirects Wesley to Alex's collage. Sumner's response is immediate, "The old adage is true, you can never go home again, I guess in this case you'd have to find a new one. I certainly hope these families have found theirs, and the happiness that goes along with it."

Sheri then explains the purpose of the pictorial, saying, "We're trying to reach some form of consensus regarding daily activity, hoping it'll point us in the right direction, while---."

Wesley begins fingering through a few loose photographs, and then stops Sheri in the middle of his sentence, saying, "You can't bring the town back, it's gone!" Sheri now feels nothing more can be accomplished through the rehashing of old dialogue and dismisses the exercise allowing each man to return to their duties.

Sheri now entertains the thought of calling Sumner back later on in the day, then realizes he hasn't any questions to ask. He then walks over to a nearby window hoping for a little inspiration, then out of the corner of his eye he sees an eagle perching itself on an isolated limb in a nearby pine tree. As the bird turns its head in an attempt to register what's below he suddenly sweeps down and snares a rabbit making its way across the yard. Sheri cringes as the large bird makes off with its prey. Then, at that precise moment he's able to interpret the eagle in Longshadow's vision.

Moments later he yells out, "Alex, where the hell are you?"

Alex hears a faint call coming from inside the building and rushes in through the rear entrance, saying, "What's going on?"

Sheri displays a gratifying grin as he says, "I've just solved one part of your grandfather's vision!" Alex eagerly listens as Sheri explains, "A little while ago an eagle flew down and across the backyard, making off with a rabbit. Anyway while I was marveling at the bird's agility, and the vision needed to spot such an animal, I came to only one conclusion, Longshadow's eagle has to be an airplane!"

Alex displays an indifferent manner by rolling his eyes then he finally says, "Suppose you're right. What then, how does this revelation fit into the equation?"

Sheri then exclaims, "Don't you see, airplanes take aerial photographs because companies and municipalities need a visual record. We need to find out if any photo's had been taken of Stockland."

Alex's enthusiasm is apparent as he says, "We've hit pay dirt, you know what this means, our search is over, instead of snapshots we'll have the entire picture!"

Although the aerial photographs are still but a promise Sheri begins to wonder what he's to expect as this drama unfolds. Then he says, "Hold on my friend, they're plenty of unknowns out there, first we'll have to locate the pictures, and then see if copies can be made. You know, we maybe opening a Pandora's box that neither of us are prepared for." With a reasonable amount of caution being displayed Sheri decides to telephone Richard that evening, hoping he'll know how to access the needed photographs.

Sheri returns to the den around seven-thirty in the evening and telephones Richard, saying, "I'm sorry you've been disturbed, but this is important. I need your help locating a set of aerial photographs that may have been taken of Stockland." Then Sheri describes Longshadow's vision and the connection he's made.

Richard then informs Sheri if the photo's had been taken, they would-be in Stockland's inventory, and are probably being kept by the Delphi's planning commission because the two towns had been incorporated soon after the Stockland properties had been abandoned. He then concludes their conversation saying he'd look into the matter in the morning and would report back as soon as he found something.

That night as Sheri tries to fall asleep he feels agitated, because things are once again being left to providence and he'll have to wait. However he does realize there's light at the end of the tunnel and with that insight he's finally able to sleep.

Chapter Seventeen

While Alex is preparing breakfast the following morning he quizzes Sheri about the telephone call he made to post, and is instructed to say nothing about the photographs. Sheri feels they're too many uncertainties at this point, and wants to avoid any unnecessary disappointments. He then goes on to say if the prints are found both he and Alex would review the material beforehand due to the complexity of the situation. With both men in agreement each proceeds with his daily routine.

Around four o'clock that afternoon Sheri receives an unexpected telephone call from Post, with him saying, "I'm the bearer of good news, my people have located the industrial negatives in Delphi's Public Works Department. Then I was informed their dimensions were thirty-six inches square, leaving me wondering how anything like that could be reproduced. However I was surprised to learn they could print the copies off their blueprint machine. Anyway they'll be rolled up and packed in storage tubes, you'll have great resolution. Oh, I almost forgot, they've offered overnight delivery, you'll have the prints sometime tomorrow."

Sheri has an awe-struck tone in his voice as he ends his conversation with Richard, then turning to Alex he exclaims, "The photos are ours, all that's left is the waiting!" He then takes the time to explain were they were found, and how the copies would-be made. Then both men go about their duties in quiet anticipation of the next day's delivery.

The following morning arrives along with the anticipation of the photos. Then just before noon a knock comes from the front door, it's a man with the photographs. Sheri takes possession of the prints and watches as the courier drives away. He now diverts attention away from himself by hiding the four tubes in a nearby closet, hoping he and Alex could study them later on after Burtrom and Wesley had left on their scheduled trip to the trading post.

Two hours later Alex is found seated at the second floor window watching Burtrom and Wesley as they leave the Lodge, then he gives Sheri the go ahead to recover the photos. Now displaying unbridled enthusiasm they rush into the den where Sheri removes the end cap from the first tube. Unrolling its contents they see for the first time what's been hidden for so many years. As this journey of tears begins to reveal itself a foreboding sensation takes hold of each man. Alex begins to feel uncomfortable, and says, "It's as if the photograph is trying to say something!"

Sheri realizes each print is exhibiting different characteristics with varying degrees of intensity, and replies, "You're right, photographs do tell a story, and we need someone who'll be able to interpret them."

Alex hasn't a clue as to how that's to be achieved, and says, "Well college boy it looks like our backs are against the wall, because there's no one around here that can accomplish that feat!"

Sheri displays his notorious grin and then replies, "Oh yes there is, and it's going to be John O'Daly." He then goes on to explain that before John entered the seminary he was an intelligence officer for the military with his specialty being in aerial reconnaissance. And if he knew his services were once again in demand he would jump at the chance to help out.

That evening Sheri places a telephone call into O'Daly's private residence, where John makes an unconscious attempt at reestablishing his authority in the matter, saying, "Sheri I'm in the middle of my dinner. As I've said in the past, if you're in need of help, telephone Post, Waters or for that matter Farmsworth. You'll have to do what's needed to get the job done, and if someone has the talent and doesn't cooperate, inform him it's his duty. Otherwise it'll be me they'll be answering to!"

Sheri finally baits his trap, by asking, "John, you're absolutely sure I'm to handle it this way?"

O'Daly's gruff voice reaffirms his position, "Certainly, and furthermore whoever refuses they're to report to me, and I'll deal with the culprit!"

With O'Daly once again cornered Sheri takes pleasure in saying, "He may end up being your worst enemy."

O'Daly yells out in a demanding tone, "Who the hell is he?"

Sheri displays a boyish smile as he replies, "It's you."

O'Daly concedes to Sheri's position, saying, "What do I have to do, and why is it so important?" Sheridan goes on to explain how the aerial photographs were found, and without his help they would- be lost for a lack of an interpretation. With a better understanding of the situation John agrees he's the best man for the job.

The next morning O'Daly clears his calendar and finally is en route to the Lodge by mid- afternoon. The trip is one of anticipation, if the truth were known John enjoyed working for the intelligence agency while serving in Korea, and this occasion would- be the perfect opportunity to put those skills back into service. He too realizes his new responsibilities could create a possible conflict, however he's unable to identify the source and dismisses the exercise in favor of a warm welcome that's waiting for him at the Lodge.

Later that afternoon as John walks through the front doorway of the retreat he's greeted by Sheri who says, "Burtrom and Wesley were told your visit was solely for the purpose of rest and relaxation. There isn't a need to explain anything, they'll be plenty of time for that later, after you've had a chance to review the photographs. With both men in agreement they join the others who are about to feast on a pork roast dinner worthy of any connoisseur.

An hour later with their appetites well satisfied the men redirect their attention. Burtrom and Wesley find comfort in the game room, while Alex tends to his duties in the kitchen. Sheri on the other hand sees an opportunity, and pulls O'Daly aside requesting they get a preliminary start by arranging the aerial photographs in the order of their importance. O'Daly enters the den and says, "There's been a few changes since my last visit, it's more reminiscent of my office in Korea." John scans the room and is taken back in time when he had performed some of the most sensitive reconnaissance work in that part of the world helping to stabilize the region. He's now startled with the sound of paper being unrolled and realizes Sheri is arranging the prints in chronological order. O'Daly seems embarrassed as he says, "I'm sorry about that, I was somewhere else, although it seemed as if it were just yesterday."

Sheri has completed his task and now motions to the prints while explaining, "As you'll see I've displayed these prints using the contours of the river as my bench mark, thereby giving us a complete perspective of the community." O'Daly now has an understanding of the demographics and what's expected of him, and instructs Sheridan to catalog each street with the number of houses or buildings to that specific area being studied. Then he's to calculate the distances between each building, and from street to street, using the scale of measurement provided at the bottom of each print as his formula.

On Wednesday morning while making their last computation O'Daly suggests reviewing their checklist for any omissions. Forty minutes into the exercise John says to Sheri, "Look at the second print, right here along the river, directly behind the Pyxis Oil Company's property line. There's an oil barge and it seems to be off loading into the above ground storage tanks."

Sheri retains his objectivity by asking, "John, how can we be sure the barge is off loading?"

O'Daly's response is so confident there's a chuckle that comes along with it as he says, "My boy we're dealing with a transfer terminal with its product destined for upstate New York." Sheri yields a puzzling look, demonstrating he's still not satisfied. O'Daly realizes Sheri's lack of expertise, and patiently continues by saying, "Notice the barge and its relationship to the crib, well the tugboat is positioned behind the barge nudging it Northward enabling the crew to tie off. You can even see the boat's wake as she's pushing. Now, if you want more evidence look at the waterline on the barge, it's clearly riding low in the water, all of which means one thing, the barge has just arrived!"

With a sense of resolve John turns to Sheri and says, "You'd better get your boy in here there's a long session ahead of us. And while you're at it ask Alex to prepare sandwiches and coffee, we'll have lunch right here!"

Sheri has already informed Alex of O'Daly's instructions, and has returned to the den with Wesley. With everyone now comfortably seated, John begins his inquiry of Sumner, saying, "Wesley we've been withholding these prints from you and Burtrom until we could get a feel for the situation. With that objective now being met I want you to tell us what it was like to haul product out of the Pyxis Tank Farm."

Wesley seems somewhat intimidated by the question, however after a moment of composure he's finally able to say, "Drivers would first pick up a blank loading ticket from the Pyxis office, and then return to their trucks and drive over to the loading- rack. Then a static-cable was connected to the trailer essentially grounding the equipment to the earth, thereby preventing an explosion. You see when static electricity comes in contact with the fumes a reaction takes place igniting the vapors. Anyway after the grounding cable is secured the driver would insert the ticket into a meter which would then register the product being transferred. Then the driver would climb on top of the trailer, place the fill-pipe into an open hole and stand there while the trailer was being loaded, all the while coping with the fumes that were coming from the trailer. It wasn't easy because the entire procedure took forty minutes to complete. The driver would finally deliver a copy of the bill of lading to the office, return to his tractor-trailer with his copy and then drive off."

Silence now fills the room as Sumner's account draws to an end. Then O'Daly encourages him to continue by saying, "Wes we need to understand the process after you left the tank farm." After a moment of reflection Sumner resumes his narrative, "Then of course we'd off-load the product either by gravity to storage tanks below the ground, such as gas stations or by means of pumps usually situated at above ground storage facilities. Then there were tractors equipped with power take off units that allowed the driver to transfer product from his transport trailer through a hose to the P.T.O. unit attached to the undercarriage of the truck and then to above ground storage."

O'Daly continues his inquiry by asking, "How many times a day would you go through these procedures?"

Wesley is slow to respond, "Usually twice, other times when hauling J.P.-4 military jet fuel for the government it would-be five or six times a day." At this point Wesley decides to register a complaint, saying, "There's one thing that really bothers me, there was never any recognition coming from the Defense Department for our contribution to national security. It was our delivery of jet fuel to the Air Force that allowed their fighters to scramble and intercept the aggressive threat of the Soviet Bear

Bomber over the Northeast corridor during the cold war. The U.S. Pilots were at minimal risk when compared to the transport driver who could had gone up in an inferno at any time while handling that stuff." Wesley hesitates for a moment then gives an example, saying, "Let's say there was a faulty static line grounding the trailer, or a static discharge coming from a driver's pants, or shoes that would had been enough to ignite the fumes. At that point there wasn't any chance of escaping the inferno." Sumner is clearly agitated with the subject matter and continues on to say, "We spent years distinguishing ourselves by taking all the risks, while those damn rocket jockeys and their superior's were patting one another on the back for a job well done. Then the Defense Department comes along and hands out ribbons and promotion for just being there. We were the one's loading up, and making the next flight possible. In short, if our tractor-trailers didn't roll those birds didn't have a chance in hell of getting off the ground. They would had rusted right there on the flight line!"

O'Daly is now concerned with Wesley's physical health at that time, and asks, "How did you feel while all this was going on?"

Sumner gives a brief reply and then offers an anecdotal account, saying, "I suffered from wicked headaches, and was tired most of the time, but I figured it was all stress related." He then suddenly yields to a puzzling expression then looks directly at O'Daly and asks, "Why would a Pyxis's employee stop me from driving away from the terminal, and then demand that I sign a medical release?"

O'Daly takes a deep breath while reaching for the telephone, then glances in Sheridan direction saying, "Would you and Wes please find Alex and let him know we'll be eating lunch in the kitchen."

The moment's that followed have a sense of urgency to them as O'Daly places a telephone call into Richard's office. Then with pleasantries lasting only a few short minutes John begins to brief Post on his findings, saying, "It looks like our efforts are paying off. From what I've been able to piece together it appears that Pyxis International Oil and Gas Company is probably behind Burtrom and Wesley's problems, and with some degree of certainty, Stockland's demise. Now listen, there seems to be a connection between gasoline and military J.P.-4 jet fuel having a toxic effect on the community. Whatever it is I want to know by Friday evening!" Richard knows O'Daly wants results and with little time to spare both men end the conversation.

O'Daly has a clearer insight as to the problem and realizes his burden will become heavier as time goes on. Then he'll certainly be required to demonstrate the connection between toxic exposure and it's effect on humanity not to mention the influence it has on man's immortal soul. This will transcend all belief systems he thinks, having a direct impact on the denominational and secular communities.

John begins to slouch in the wooden swivel chair he's been sitting in, and seems to go into a self-hypnotic trance. Then a few moments later he sits in an upright fashion and slides the center desk drawer open. Now he withdraws a manila folder and begins to write down (Hell's Kitchen) as the code name for this cryptic operation.

John leaves his temporary office hoping he'll find some measure of relief while in the company of the other men who are now waiting for him in the kitchen. However with an air of anxiety filling the room O'Daly feels a change would-be in everyone's best interest, and announces, "I want to thank all of you for working so hard on this project." He now looks in Hunter's direction, while asking, "Would it be too much of a bother if we refrigerate this meal?" Alex smiles and then stores the food away. Now with everyone waiting around John says, "In appreciation of everyone's efforts I want to treat you boys to lunch. How about that little place down the road, Buck's, is it?"

It's every man for himself, with the activity all reminiscent of a 1930's comedy sketch, with each going in different directions, accomplishing whatever needs to be done in order to go. And within ten minutes they're all en route to Bucks, far away from the stress and problems that's afflicted each man since the onset of this project.

As the afternoon hours eclipse one another camaraderie replaces the guarded demeanor each man had displayed earlier. With their palates awash with coffee the remainder of the afternoon takes on the characteristics of a Celebrity Roast, with each ridiculing the other in a way that's thoroughly entertaining. As in all cases when one enjoys the company there in time passes far too quickly, and with a need to return the men drive back to the Lodge arriving there sometime after seven o'clock. With appetites well satisfied each man now seeks out comfort in one way or the other hoping it'll dispel the chill of this December evening.

Sheri selects the game room for it's warmth, and invites Alex and John to join him, saying, "You know John I've been watching you since Sunday, and I must say I'm quite impressed with your style. You have a natural talent for this sort of thing, there must be a reason why you choose your present vocation over that of an operative."

O'Daly needs to put this issue behind him, and says, "There was too much going on at that time, and with the political winds being so unpredictable I decided to resign my commission when my tour was completed and return to New York."

With both men feeling uncomfortable with the topic Alex changes it, by saying, "It's been a long day and before going to sleep I want to know where this Stockland issue stands."

O'Daly places his feet on a nearby coffee table in a matter of fact way, saying, "My money's on poisonous emissions, with a possible conspiracy or two along the way."

Alex seems enthralled by the statement, and replies, "You're able to come to that conclusion just from looking at those aerial photographs?"

O'Daly is quite confident in his appraisal, and says, "It's only a conjecture, however all that will change after we connect the dots. That'll be the easy part because all the indicators are there, and they're in black and white for everyone to see!"

Sheri is fascinated with John's intuitive nature, and says, "Don't leave us dangling, connect a few of those dots so we're able to see what's going on."

John then explains how the images can be interrupted into events, saying, "The aerial prints reveal more than casual activity. It appears Pyxis International Oil and Gas Company had a transfer terminal in Stockland where products like gasoline, and jet fuel were stored in large quantities, waiting for shipment. I could tell from the photo's that barges capable of holding 10.000 barrels would tie-up, make their connection, and then pump off their product into above ground storage tanks. All the while allowing the fumes to aerosol into the community. And with inhabitants being a stone's throw away, the town would have been in peril most of the time. Then, if you factor in product being transferred into rail-car and tractor trailers, then the citizenry received compound exposures."

The issue of wind direction still isn't clear in Alex's mind and he wants to know how that determination was made, "How can you be so certain in what direction the wind was blowing while all this was going on?"

O'Daly responds to the challenge, by saying, "The resolution on the prints are exceptionally clear, you can see two flags, one at the Pyxis Oil Company's office, and the other in front of Stockland's Town Hall. Both are flying in the same direction, toward the community." O'Daly turns to Sheri, and says, "Today's December 2nd, Friday evening Richard will

251

telephone with an update on what he's been able to learn with respect those properties in gasoline and jet fuel. Your task from that point on will be to determine how these chemicals affect the human physiology. Hit the books, and burn as much midnight oil as possible." Both men recognize the unconscious pun, and smile, then O'Daly continues, "If you require special textbooks from the library ask Brian Farmsworth, he'll pick them up and deliver them to you personally. In any event, I want your report by Sunday morning. Now, with that said you boys better get some sleep, the clock is ticking."

The next day Sheri telephones Brian and informs him of O'Daly's instructions, and asks that he do a literary search on gasoline and jet fuel. Brian now displays interest in the clandestine operation and then assures Sheri he'll locate the needed textbooks, and find coverage for his weekend duties.

The following days pass with anticipation and mixed emotions, its only after Brian's arrival on Friday does the pace pick-up. With textbooks in hand Sheri retreats to his room and begins preparing for the upcoming thirty-six hour marathon.

That evening everyone waits in anticipation for this prearranged conference call to take place, then at eight-twenty the telephone rings, with O'Daly answering, "Hold on Richard I'm going to switch over to the speaker phone."

Richard is now confident he's met his obligation to O'Daly, and says, "You boys are dealing with a real hazardous situation. Matter of fact some of the constituents of gasoline and J.P.-4 jet fuel can produce a psychedelic effect in both animals and humans. My sources also tell me that populations living near storage facilities like Pyxis are at a higher risk, the principle cause being the aerosolizing of petroleum products into the community while the loading and unloading process is taking place."

John pauses just long enough to collect his thoughts and then asks, "Dick would this apply to gas stations too?"

Post responds, "Any station without a complete vapor-recovery system would produce the same effect. One thing worth noting, when the humidity's high it keeps those toxic chemicals closer to the ground. In the case of Pyxis, the storage capacity was in the millions of gallons, that risk was certainly compounded. I might add unburnt' fuel emissions coming from automobiles and trucks have a toxic effect too."

With O'Daly's facial features now expressing anger his commanding voice is asking, "How long has this been going on?"

Richard replies, "It's interesting you've brought that up, another source of mine in Texas tells me Pyxis and others knew about the danger of these chemicals as far back as the 1940's. The military on the other hand had formulated J.P.-4 in the beginning of the 1950's, and made wide use of it through the early 1980's. From where I'm sitting there's been an attempt to keep this information from the general public. It'll take time but history will be rewritten along with a few medical texts." As their conversation ends, O'Daly praises Richard for his diligence.

The stillness within the room seems to reflect the mood of each man. No one had been prepared for the tragedy that's been revealed. The consensus prior to this evening was that Stockland had been an isolated situation, but to include the United States along with the rest of the world that's unfathomable. As the shock begins to ware off Sheri is the first to repeat one of Richard's comments, "That psychedelic effect Dick spoke of certainly would explain Wesley's and William Case's addiction to alcohol. Then you would have to consider all drivers and mechanics, not to mention other inadequate diagnoses similar to that of Keno's."

O'Daly is clearly disturbed by this report, and says, "Not only that, but think of all those unsuspecting men, women, and children that had an untold misery inflicted upon them pursuing the American dream. Pyxis certainly placed an unseen obstacle in their path, I guess you could say the operative word here is unseen."

John knows what's expected of Sheri, and says, "Well my boy, you better get some sleep, remember I'll be looking for your report early Sunday morning." As Sheridan leaves in the direction of his room, O'Daly along with Alex are in pursuit of theirs.

An atmosphere of tranquillity sets the tone for that Saturday. Alex goes about performing his duties almost in a traumatized state with the dialogue of last evening's conversation still fresh in his mind. He then wonders why corporations would willfully place the lives of so many people in peril without warning them of the consequences. Then on a lighter note Burtrom and Wesley find solace reviewing the aerial prints, identifying different landmarks, while reflecting on events that took place so many years ago.

O'Daly on the other hand draws on his intestinal fortitude, and occupies Saturday on the telephone networking in an attempt to develop a coalition that would address this issue.

While at the same time knowing it would take more than just he and a few others if they were going to be successful in their quest.

Chapter Eighteen

Sheridan is startled into consciousness Sunday morning after napping for two hours and realizes it's nearly nine o'clock. He dresses and then walks downstairs and into the kitchen where he pours a cup of coffee. Sheri now develops the confidences he'll be needing, and then walks into the den. O'Daly, who's been waiting, looks up at Sheridan, and says, "You could of taken a few minutes and made yourself a little more presentable."

Sheri sips on his coffee and then sits down in an adjacent chair to where O'Daly is sitting, and says, "John you ordered me to this task, it's been completed, and per your request a report is to be made. They'll be plenty of time to cleanup afterwards. As for now I want everyone in here, and would you please ask

Alex to brew up a fresh pot of coffee, I've had only four hours sleep since Friday and I need to stay awake." O'Daly isn't about to argue for he knows Sheridan is holding the cards. Fifteen minutes later O'Daly returns with the coffeepot and the men.

Although Sheri looks as if he's pulled an all-nighter in preparation for final examines he's still able to address his audience, saying, "The volume of material I've uncovered was so overwhelming it seems futile to even discuss those cases in their entirety. So I'll sum up everything that I've read, hoping you'll make the connection." With all eyes fixed, Sheri continues, "The sources of exposure would come from vapors in their fumed or aerosol state, notably in the form of gasoline, and J.P.-4 jet fuel. They would then pass through the sinus cavity and go directly to the brain and interact with the central nervous system. Which would then leave most individuals with serious neurological complications compromising their quality of health. I might add there's no escaping the complex carnage due to the principal of causation." With everyone waiting Sheri finishes his coffee then continues with the report saying, "You could say the residents of Stockland were going around in a slightly altered state of consciousness. Which translates into a perception of reality far different from other populations who have never been exposed to toxic chemicals. In conclusion, if conditions were this bad here, what are they like in the Third World?"

There's a somber mood airing throughout the room as Sheri refills his coffee cup. He then walks over to a nearby window through which he's able to see Longshadow's cabin standing high above the shoreline. He now watches a Thunderbird, which was thought to have been extinct, riding the wind currents in a slow circular pattern above the building. As if safeguarding the old man's spirit. As the bird eclipses the sunlight Sheri emits an enlighten smile, indicating he's finally able to understand the vision, and acknowledges to himself that each man can cast a long shadow, if whatever he does is for the betterment of mankind. Now with the Epiphany over he rejoins the others.

Epilogue

As these people slept, a formless spirit from the deepest bowels of the earth emerged and embraced their lifeless forms taking possession of each unsuspecting body through the expressionless orifices of their countenances, while ravaging their sacred souls forevermore.

The End

David J. Miller

Revised and changed from A Priest and the Spirits Down Under to HELL'S KITCHEN   (From where everyone is served)

Author's Bio

David Miller received his secondary education from Rice Memorial High School in South Burlington, Vermont and has been Jeffersonian educated at the master's level. David has distinguished himself in the field of Aromatic Hydrocarbons researching the subject matter for nearly 10 years. He has written a medical commentary which acted as a catalyst for the state of Vermont Department of Health, division of Health Protection, Environmental Health to issue a facts sheet on benzene. David also was a co-presenter at the 16th regional cancer research symposium held on Oct. 19, 20th, 2000, and has preformed the duties of evaluator and lecturer at the university level.